# THE PORCUPINE

# THE
# PORCUPINE
# JULIAN
# BARNES

ALFRED A. KNOPF    NEW YORK    1992

*To Dimitrina*

THIS IS A BORZOI BOOK
PUBLISHED BY ALFRED A. KNOPF, INC.

Copyright © 1992 by Julian Barnes

All rights reserved under International and Pan-
American Copyright Conventions. Published in the
United States by Alfred A. Knopf, Inc., New York.
Distributed by Random House, Inc., New York.
Published in Great Britain by Jonathan Cape Limited,
London.

ISBN 0-679-41917-9
LC 92-54773

Manufactured in the United States of America
Published November 20, 1992
Third Printing, December 1992

# THE PORCUPINE

THE OLD MAN stood as close to the sixth-floor window as the soldier would allow. Outside, the city was abnormally dark; inside, the low wattage of the desk lamp slid thinly from the metal rim of his heavy spectacles. He was less spruce than the militiaman had expected: the suit had corrugations at the back, and what remained of his sandy hair lurched up in tufts. But his posture was confident; there was even belligerence in the way his left foot was placed firmly on the painted line. With head slightly cocked, the old man listened as the women's protest wound through the tight centre of the capital he had bossed for so long. He smiled to himself.

They had gathered on this damp December evening in front of the Cathedral of St Michael the Archangel, a rallying point from the old days of the monarchy. Many went inside first and lit candles at shoulder height: thin, yellow candles which had a tendency, either from poor manufacture or the heat of the surrounding flames, to bend at the waist as they burned, dropping their beeswax with a soft splash into the swimming tray beneath. Then the women, each armed with

I

her weapons of protest, came out into the cathedral square which until so recently had been forbidden them, had been ringed by troops under the command of an officer in a leather coat with no visible rank. Here the darkness was concentrated, for in this sector only one street-lamp in six gave out its exhausted glow. Many of the women now reached for stouter, whiter candles. To save every match but the first, each new candle was lit from the flame of another.

Though some wore fur-fabric coats, most had come dressed according to instructions. Or rather, not dressed: they looked as if they had just arrived from the kitchen. Aprons tied over thick print dresses, with a heavy sweater originally pulled on against an unheated apartment now serving to combat the chill in the cathedral square. Into the deep placket of her apron, or into her coat pocket if more formally clad, each woman had stuck a large kitchen implement: an aluminium ladle, a wooden spoon, occasionally a sharpening steel or even, as if at some level a note of menace was required, a weighty carving fork.

The demonstration began at six o'clock, the hour when the women were traditionally in the kitchen preparing the dinner, although lately this word had come to stand for a fevered concoction, somewhere between a broth and a stew, made from a couple of turnips, a chicken neck if you could find one, a few leaves, water and stale bread. Tonight they would not be stirring this shameful gruel with the ladles and spoons they carried in their pockets. Tonight they took these implements out and waved them at one another with a little self-conscious excitement. Then they began.

As the organisers, a group of six women from the

2

Metalurg complex (block 328, staircase 4), left the cobbled square and took their first steps on to the tarmacked boulevard with its two sets of darkly shining tramlines, the first aluminium ladle was struck against its saucepan. For a few moments, as others joined in with respectful timidity, the noise kept a slow, pausing beat, an eery funeral music of the kitchen. But when the bulk of the protesters took up the call, those first instants of solemn order disappeared, the silences were filled with the sound of new strikings from the rear, until the precincts of the cathedral, where people now came openly to seek God in quiet prayer, were crammed with urgent domestic noise.

Those inside the demonstration could distinguish from nearby the different notes that were being struck: the dead, dully echoing sound of aluminium on aluminium, the higher, more martial cry of wood on aluminium, the surprisingly light mess-time call of wood on iron, and the heavy, road-mending sound of aluminium upon iron. The noise grew fat, and huddled over the women as they set off, a noise none in the city had ever heard before, one made more potent by its strangeness and lack of rhythm; it was insistent, oppressive, sharper than mourning. A group of young men at the first corner shouted obscenities and raised stiff forearms; but the grand clatter reduced them to hopeless fish-mouths, and their insults reached no further than the jaundiced burn of their street-lamp.

The organisers had expected at most a few hundred women from the Metalurg complex. But the rampant noise which followed the glinting curves of Tramway 8 came from several thousand: from Youth and Hope and Friendship, from Red Star, Gagarin and Future Victory, even from Lenin and Red Army. Those with candles held them in the socket of their

3

thumb, with their fingers gripping the cooking pot or frying pan they had brought; and when the spoon or ladle held in the other hand came down upon the pan the flame of the candle shivered and grease sprayed over their sleeves. They carried no banners and shouted no slogans: that was what men did. They offered instead a battery of metallic noise and a sunflower field of yellow faces lit by candles which jumped at every drum stroke.

The women came out of Stanov Street and into the Square of the People, where the damp cobbles mocked them like a vast tray of shiny buns. They reached the squat, bomb-proof Mausoleum which held the embalmed corpse of the First Leader; but the demonstration did not pause there, nor did its volume of sound increase. It crossed the square in front of the Archaeological Museum, boldly skirted the requisitioned Office of State Security, where the old man strained and smiled and inched his foot against the white line, then rounded the elegant neo-classical palace which until recently had been the headquarters of the Communist Party. Several windows on the ground floor were now filled in with hardboard, and at the angle of the building an act of enthusiastic if minor arson had left a spreading swipe of black from the second to the seventh floor. But the women did not pause even here, except for some of them to spit – a practice which had begun cautiously a year or so ago, became a national necessity for a while so that the fire brigade would be called to hose down the cobbles at the end of each day, but which now had begun to decline in popularity. Even so, enough women chose to express their contempt for the Socialist (formerly Communist) Party to make those at the back skid on the spumed stones.

The steady domestic noise, the sound of national keening

4

and empty stomachs, passed the Sheraton Hotel, where the rich foreigners stayed; some of the guests stood expectantly at their windows, holding the candles they had been advised to bring, candles of a better quality than those in the street below. When they understood the cause of the protest, some drew back into their rooms, reflecting on the food they had idly left on their plates at breakfast: small cubes of local white cheese, a couple of olives, half an apple, a teabag used only once. The memory of their unthinking profligacy set off a brief match-flare of guilt.

The women now had only a short way to go until they reached the parliament building, where they expected to be stopped by militiamen. But the soldiers, daunted by the advancing noise, had already retreated behind the large iron gates, which they had locked, leaving outside only two of their number, one in each sentry-box. The guards were young conscripts from the eastern province, with brutally fresh haircuts and limited political understanding; each held a sub-machine gun horizontally across his chest and gazed sternly above the women's heads as if contemplating a distant ideal.

But the women in turn ignored the soldiers. They had not come for an exchange of insults, for provocation and the lick of martyrdom. They halted a dozen yards before the sentry-boxes, and those behind did not press dangerously forward. Such discipline contrasted with the thunderous cacophony they produced, a beating, throbbing, dinning, hungry sound which reached its full density as the last protesters packed into the square. The noise eased through the railings in front of the parliament building, stalked up the broad steps and battered down the gilded double doors. It respected no procedural laws or rules of debate as it clattered into the

Chamber of Deputies, imposing itself upon a discussion of land reform and forcing a representative of the Peasants' Agricultural Party to abandon his speech and return to his desk. The deputies were brightly lit, thanks to their emergency power supply, and for the first time embarrassed by their visibility; they sat in silence, occasionally glancing at one another and shrugging as the enormous protest, which contained no words but every argument, invaded the place where they worked. Outside the women beat their spoons and ladles on cooking pots and frying pans, wood on aluminium, wood on iron, aluminium on iron, aluminium upon itself. The candles had burnt down and the wax now splashed hotly on the thumbs that gripped them, but the noise and the flickering lights continued. There was no decline into words, for they had heard nothing but words and words and words – inedible, indigestible words – for months and months and months. They spoke with metal, though not with the metal that usually spoke on such occasions, the metal that left martyrs. They spoke without words, they argued, bellowed, demanded and reasoned without words, they pleaded and wept without words. They did so for an hour, and then, at eight o'clock, as if by a secret signal, they began to leave the square in front of the parliament building. They did not stop their noise, however; instead, the great hump of sound shook itself like an ox climbing to its feet. Then the protesters began to disperse from the city centre towards the apartment complexes beyond the boulevards: back to Metalurg and Gagarin, Red Star and Future Victory. The noise jangled down the broader avenues, clinked into alleyways, diminishing as it went; occasionally, at street corners, it would bang into itself again, startled and tinny, like a pair of cheap cymbals.

6

The old man on the sixth floor of the requisitioned Office of State Security was now at his deal table, eating a pork chop and reading that morning's *Truth*. He heard a segment of din coming back towards him from the direction of the Socialist (formerly Communist) Party headquarters. He stopped eating to note its clattering approach, its inchoate climax, its leaking departure. The old man's face was fully lit by the desk lamp. The militiaman on duty three metres away assumed that Stoyo Petkanov was smiling at a cartoon in the newspaper.

*

Peter Solinsky and his wife Maria lived in a small apartment in the Friendship complex (block 307, staircase 2) north of the boulevards. He had been offered larger accommodation when appointed Prosecutor General, but turned it down. For the moment, anyway: it hardly seemed tactful to accept any visible favour from the new government while charging its predecessor with massive abuse of privilege. Maria found this argument absurd. The Prosecutor General should not live in a law professor's dingy three-room mouse-hole and expect his wife to use the bus. Besides, the place had almost certainly been bugged at some stage by the security police. She had had enough of their conversations and, God only knew, their occasional love-making being listened to by some thick-faced oaf in a mildewed basement.

Solinsky had ordered the apartment to be swept. The two men in short leather coats shook their heads knowingly as they unscrewed the telephone; but their small discovery did not satisfy Maria. They had probably planted it themselves in the first place, she commented. And of course there were

7

more: the one in the telephone was the sort you were intended to find and then imagine you were safe. But there would always be somebody interested in knowing what the Prosecutor General talked about when he got home from the office. In which case, Peter had argued, any new apartment we move into will probably have the very latest equipment installed, so what advantage would that be?

However, there was another reason why Peter Solinsky preferred to stay where he had lived for the last nine years. The windows of the even-numbered apartments of their block faced north, towards a low range of hills which according to military theorists had formed a useful defence against the Dacians when the city had been founded a couple of millennia ago. On the nearest eminence, which Peter could just make out above a layer of thickened and slowly churning air, stood the Statue of Eternal Gratitude to the Liberating Red Army. A heroic bronze soldier, left foot advancing steadfastly, head fixed nobly high, and higher still a brandished rifle with sparkling bayonet. Around the plinth bronze machine-gunners in bas-relief defended their position with principled ferocity.

Solinsky had visited the statue often as a child, when his father had still been favoured. A plump and serious boy in his starched Red Pioneer's uniform, he would always be roused by the ritual on Liberation Day, as on the Day of the October Revolution, and the Day of the Soviet Army. The brass band, gleaming more brightly than the bronze bayonet prodding the sky, disgorged its sombre music. The Soviet Ambassador and the Commander of the Fraternal Soviet Forces laid wreaths as big as tractor tyres, and were followed by the President and the Head of the Patriotic Defence Forces; then all four retreated together, shoulder to shoulder awkwardly, as if fearing a sudden step behind them. Each year Peter had felt flattered and grown-up; each year he had believed more headily in solidarity between the socialist nations, in their progress, in their inevitable, scientific victory.

Until a few years ago, couples on their wedding day often made a pilgrimage to Alyosha, as he was known; they would stand beneath him, all tears and roses, overcome by the grave momentary connection between the personal and the historic. In recent years, this habit had died away, until the only visitors, except on specific days of celebration, were Russian tourists. Perhaps, as they dropped a few flowers on the plinth, they felt virtuous, imagining the gratitude of the liberated nations.

The morning and evening sun spotlit the distant Alyosha for the city. Peter Solinsky liked to sit at his small desk by the window and wait until he sensed a tremor of light on the soldier's bayonet. Then he would look up and think: that's what has been stuck in the guts of my country for nearly fifty years. Now it was his job to help pull it out.

*

The accused in Criminal Law Case Number 1 had been informed that a preliminary meeting with Prosecutor General Solinsky would take place at ten o'clock. Stoyo Petkanov was therefore awake at six, preparing his tactics and his demands. It was important never to yield the initiative.

That first morning of his incarceration, for instance. They had arrested him, quite illegally, without mentioning any charges, and brought him to the Office of State Security, which they had given some new bourgeois name. A senior militiaman had shown him a bed and a table, pointed out a

9

semicircular white line on the floor round the window, and then handed him some confetti. That, at any rate, was how he had thought of it, and how he had treated it.

'What is this?' he had asked, tossing the sheets of coloured tickets on to the table.

'Those are your ration coupons.'

'So, you are kindly permitting me to go out and queue up?'

'Prosecutor General Solinsky has decided that since you are now an ordinary citizen you will naturally be subject to the temporary stringencies which all ordinary citizens are undergoing.'

'I see . . . So, what exactly must I do?' Petkanov enquired, in a facsimile of senile submission. 'What am I allowed?'

'These are your coupons for cheese, these for yellow cheese, these for flour.' The soldier helpfully picked through the various sheets. 'Butter, bread, eggs, meat, cooking oil, washing-powder, petrol . . . '

'I shall not, I imagine, be needing the petrol.' Petkanov gave a chuckle which invited complicity. 'Perhaps you might . . . ?' But the officer was already shrinking away. 'No, I understand. And they would only add a charge of attempting to bribe a member of the Patriotic Defence Forces, wouldn't they?'

The militiaman did not reply. 'Anyway,' Petkanov continued, like someone theoretically interested in having a new game demonstrated to him, 'anyway, tell me how it works.'

'Each coupon represents a week's supply of the goods listed on the ticket. You are responsible for the rate at which you consume rationed goods.'

'What about sausages? I do not see them here. My love of sausages is well known.' He seemed more puzzled than complaining.

'There are no coupons for sausages. The fact is, sir, there are no sausages in the shops, and therefore it would be useless issuing coupons for them.'

'Logical,' replied the former President. He began tearing off one ticket from each coloured sheet. 'I will not be needing the petrol, for obvious reasons. Bring me the rest.' And he thrust the confetti at the officer.

An hour later, a soldier returned with one loaf of bread, 200 grams of butter, a small cabbage, two meatballs, 100 grams of white cheese and 100 grams of yellow cheese, half a litre of cooking oil (a month's supply), 300 grams of washing-powder (ditto) and half a kilogram of flour. Petkanov asked him to set them down on the table and bring him a knife, a fork and a glass of water. Then, beneath the formal eyes of the two militiamen, he ate the meatballs, the white cheese and the yellow cheese, the raw cabbage, the bread and the butter. He pushed back his plate, briefly eyeing the washing-powder, cooking oil and flour, then went to his narrow, iron-framed bed and lay down.

In mid-afternoon the senior militiaman returned. In some confusion, as if he himself was partly to blame, he said to the supine prisoner, 'You do not seem to have understood. As I explained . . . '

Petkanov swung his short legs on to the noisy boards and marched the few metres across to the officer. He stood very close and poked the greeny-grey uniform hard, just below the left collar-bone. Then he poked again. The militiaman stepped back, not so much from the assaulting finger as from his first true close-up of a face whose image had dominated all his previous life; a face now lifted hectoringly up at him.

'Colonel,' the former President began, 'I do not intend to use my washing-powder. I do not intend to use my cooking oil or my flour. You may have observed that I am not a *baba* in an apartment block beyond the boulevards. The people you now choose to serve may have fucked up the economy so that you all have to live with this ... *confetti.* But when you served *me*,' – he emphasised this with another hefty prod – 'when you were loyal to *me*, to the People's Socialist Republic, you will recall that there was food in the shops. You will recall that there were sometimes queues, but there was none of this shit. So you go away, and from now on you bring me socialist rations. And you can tell Prosecutor General Solinsky, first that he can go fuck himself, and second that if he wants me to eat washing-powder for the rest of the week he personally will bear the consequences.'

The officer had retreated. From then on meals arrived normally for Stoyo Petkanov. He got yoghurt as often as he requested it. Twice there had even been sausage. The former President made jokes about washing-powder to his guards, and each time food came he told himself that things were not lost, that they underestimated him at their peril.

He had also compelled them to fetch his wild geranium. At the time of his illegal arrest the soldiers had made him leave it behind. But everyone knew that Stoyo Petkanov, faithful to the soil of his nation, slept with a wild geranium beneath his bed. Everyone knew that. So after a day or two they capitulated. He had pruned the plant with his nail scissors to make it fit under his low prison bed, and ever since he had slept better.

Now he was waiting for Solinsky. He stood two metres from the window, his left foot toeing the white line. Some incompetent had attempted to paint a smooth semicircle on the pine boards, but his arm must have trembled, either from fear or drink, as he dragged his clogging brush. Were they really worried about an attempt on his life, as they claimed? If he were them he would have welcomed one, and let him stand wherever he wanted. In those first few days, whenever they took him from his room a sudden scene ran through his head: a halt by some grubby metal door in the basement, an oiled release from the handcuffs, a push in the back and a cry of 'Run!' to which he would instinctively respond, and then a final concussion. Why they hadn't done it he couldn't imagine; and their indecision gave him another reason for contempt.

He heard the militiaman's heels click as Solinsky arrived, but did not turn his head. In any case, he knew what to expect: a plump, greasy boy in a shiny Italian suit with an ingratiating expression on his face, the counter-revolutionary son of a counter-revolutionary, the shitty son of a shit. He continued gazing out of the window for a few more seconds, then said, without deigning to look round, 'So, now even your women are protesting.'

'It is their right.'

'Who next? Children? Gypsies? Mental defectives?'

'It is their right,' Solinsky repeated evenly.

'It may be their right, but what does it mean? A government that cannot keep its women in the kitchen is fucked, Solinsky, fucked.'

'Well, we shall see, shan't we?'

Petkanov nodded to himself and finally turned. 'Anyway, how are you, Peter?' He bustled across, extending his hand to the Prosecutor General. 'We haven't met for far too long. Congratulations on your . . . recent fortune.' Not a boy any more, he had to admit, and no longer plump: sallow, thinnish, neat; hair beginning to recede. For the moment he looked thoroughly at ease with himself. Well, that would change.

'We haven't met', Solinsky replied, 'since my party card was withdrawn and I was denounced in *Truth* as a fascist sympathiser.'

Petkanov laughed easily. 'It seems to have done you no harm. Or do you wish you were still in the Party today? Membership is not closed, you know.'

The Prosecutor General sat down at the table and laid his hands on a manila file in front of him. 'I understand that you have attempted to refuse legal representation.'

'Correct.' Petkanov stayed on his feet, judging this tactically advantageous.

'It would be advisable . . . '

'Advisable? I spent thirty-three years making the fucking laws, Peter, I know what they mean.'

'Nevertheless, State Advocate Milanova and State Advocate Zlatarova have been appointed by the court to act as your defence counsel.'

'More women! Tell them not to bother.'

'They are ordered to appear before the court and will act as required.'

'We shall see. And how is your father, Peter? Not too well, I hear?'

'The cancer is advanced.'

'I am sorry. You will embrace him on my behalf when next you see him.'

'I doubt it.'

The former President watched Solinsky's hands: they were thin, with black hair down to the middle knuckle; bony, fleshless fingertips pattered nervously on the pale cardboard. Deliberately, Petkanov pressed on. 'Peter,

Peter, your father and I were old comrades. How are his bees, by the way?'

'The bees?'

'Your father keeps bees, I understand.'

'Since you ask, they are sick too. Many are born without wings.'

Petkanov grunted, as if this showed ideological deviationism on their part. 'We fought the Fascists together, your father and I.'

'And then you purged him.'

'Socialism is not built without sacrifice. Your father understood that once. Before he started waving his conscience around like it was his prick.'

'You should have stopped that sentence earlier.'

'Which one?'

'*Socialism is not built.* You should have stopped there. That would have done.'

'So, do you plan to hang me? Or do you prefer the firing squad? I must ask my distinguished female defence counsel what has been decided. Or am I expected to throw myself from this window here? Is that why I'm not allowed near it until the right time?'

When Solinsky declined to reply, the former President sat down heavily opposite him. 'Whose laws are you charging me under, Peter? Your laws or my laws?'

'Oh, your laws. Your constitution.'

'And what will you find me guilty of?' The tone was brisk yet collusive.

'*I* would find you guilty of many things. Theft. Embezzlement of state funds. Corruption. Speculation. Currency offences. Profiteering. Complicity in the murder of Simeon Popov.'

'Not something I knew about. I thought he died of a heart attack, anyway.'

'Complicity in torture. Complicity in attempted genocide. Innumerable conspiracies to pervert the course of justice. What you will actually be charged with is to be announced in the next few days.'

Petkanov grunted, as if sizing up some deal on offer. 'No rape, at least. I thought that's what those women were demonstrating about, that according to Prosecutor General Solinsky I had raped them all. But I understand they were only protesting against the fact that there is now less food in the shops than at any time under Socialism.'

'I am not here', replied Solinsky stiffly, 'to discuss the difficulties inherent in the changeover from a controlled economy to a market economy.'

Petkanov chuckled. 'Congratulations, Peter. My congratulations.'

'On what?'

'That sentence. I heard your father's voice in it. Are you sure you don't want to rejoin our renamed organisation?'

'I shall talk to you next in court.'

Petkanov continued to chuckle as the prosecutor gathered up his papers and left. Then he went over to the young militiaman who had been present throughout the interview. 'Did you enjoy that, my boy?'

'I didn't hear anything,' the soldier replied implausibly.

'There are difficulties inherent in the changeover from a controlled economy to a market economy,' repeated the former President. 'There's no food in the fucking shops.'

*

Would they shoot him? Well, there were no bears in the ground. No, they probably wouldn't: they didn't have the guts. Or rather, they knew better than to make a martyr of him. Much better to discredit him. Which is what he wouldn't let them do. They would stage the trial their way, how it suited them, lying and cheating and fixing evidence, but maybe he'd have a few tricks for them too. He wasn't going to play the part allotted him. He had a different script in mind.

Nicolae. They shot him. On Christmas Day, too. Yes, but in hot blood, chased him from his palace, followed his helicopter, trailed his car, dragged him out before what they laughably called a people's court, found him guilty of murdering 60,000 people, shot him, shot them both, Nicolae and Elena, just like that, nail down the vampire, that's what someone had said, nail down the vampire before the sun sets and he learns to fly again. That's what it had been, fear. It wasn't the people's rage, or whatever they called it for the western media, it was simple brown-trousered fear. Nail him down, quick, this is Rumania, thrust a stake through his heart, nail him down. Well, there are no bears in the ground.

And then almost the first thing they'd done in Bucharest afterwards was hold a fashion show. He'd seen it on television, tarts displaying their breasts and legs, and some woman designer sneering at Elena's dress sense, telling the world how the Conducator's wife had 'bad taste' and dismissing her style as 'classical peasant'. Petkanov remembered that phrase and its intonation. So this is where we are now, which is where we were before, with snooty bourgeois whores sneering at how the proletariat dressed. What did a man need clothes for? Only to keep warm and to hide his shame. You could always tell when a comrade was showing deviationist tendencies, he would be off to Italy for a shiny suit and come back looking like a gigolo or a pederast. Just like Comrade Prosecutor General Solinsky after his fraternal visit to Turin. Yes, that had been an interesting little business. He was glad he had a memory for such things.

Gorbachev. You only had to look at the people surrounding him to see there was going to be trouble. That nose-in-the-air wife of his with her Paris frocks and American Express card and her competition for best-dressed capitalist wife with Nancy Reagan. Gorbachev couldn't even keep his own wife in line, so what chance was there of him stopping the counter-revolution once it had started? Not that he'd wanted to. You could see those gigolos he travelled with, all his advisers and special representatives and personal spokesmen who couldn't wait for their foreign trips to get some Italian tailor crawling up their legs. That spokesman, what was he called, the one the capitalists loved, he had a shiny suit. The one who said the Brezhnev Doctrine was dead. The one who said it had been replaced by the Frank Sinatra Doctrine.

That was another moment when he'd realised that everything was fucked. The Sinatra Doctrine. I did it my way. But there was only one way, one true scientific path of Marxism-Leninism. To say that the nations of the Warsaw Pact were being allowed to do things their way was as good as saying, We don't care any more about Communism, let's just hand it all over to the American bandits, fuck it all. And what a phrase to choose. The Sinatra Doctrine. Toadying to Uncle Sam like that. And who was Sinatra? Some Italian in a shiny suit who went around with the Mafia all the time. Someone Nancy Reagan went down on her knees to. Yes, that made sense. It all started with Frank Sinatra, the whole fucking thing. Sinatra fucked Nancy Reagan in the White House, that's what they said, didn't they? Reagan couldn't control his wife. Nancy had a dressing-up competition with Raisa. Gorbachev couldn't control *his* wife. And Gorbachev's spokesman says we're all going to follow the Frank Sinatra Doctrine. The Elvis Presley Doctrine. The McDonald's Hamburger Doctrine. The Doctrine of Mickey Mouse and Donald Duck.

His Department of External Security had once shown him a document passed on by their fraternal colleagues in the KGB. It was an FBI report on the safety of the American President, his levels of protection, and so forth. Petkanov always remembered one particular detail: that the place where the American President felt most safe, and where the FBI considered him most safe, was in Disneyland. No American assassin would dream of shooting him there. It would be sacrilege, it would be an offence against the great gods of Mickey Mouse and Donald Duck. This was what it had said in an FBI report conveyed to Petkanov's Department of External Security by the KGB in case such information might prove useful to them. For Petkanov it had confirmed the infantile nature of the Americans who would soon be invading his country and buying it all up. Welcome, Uncle Sam, come and build a big Disneyland here, so that your President will feel safe, and you can listen to your Frank Sinatra records and laugh at us all because you think we are ignorant peasants who don't know how to dress.

*

They had to be witnesses, Vera insisted. All four of them together: Vera, Atanas, Stefan and Dimiter. This was a great moment in their country's history, a farewell to grim child-hood and grey, fretful adolescence. It was the end of lies and illusions; now the time had arrived when truth was possible, when maturity began. How could they be absent from that?

Besides, they had been together from the start, from that recent, distant month when it had felt almost like a lark, an excuse for the boys to hang around Vera and flirt with her safely. They had gone along to those first anxious protests, uncertain what they could say, how far they could go. They had watched and marched and shouted as it had all turned serious and stiflingly passionate. Terrifying, too: they had been together when that friend of Pavel's had been half-crushed by an armoured car on Liberation Boulevard, when the militiamen guarding the presidential palace had lost their nerve and started hitting women with their rifles. Several times they had run from gunfire, shit-scared, dodging into doorways, linking arms and trying to protect Vera. But they had also been there when it had begun to feel like pushing at a loose, worm-eaten old door, when the soldiers grinned and winked at them, and shared their cigarettes. And not long afterwards they knew they were winning because even some Communist Party deputies had wanted to show their faces at the demonstrations.

'Rats jumping ship,' commented Atanas. 'Weasels.' He was a student of languages, a drinker and a poet, who liked to claim that his scepticism disinfected the germy souls of the other three.

'We can't purify the human race,' Vera told him.

'Why not?'

'There'll always be opportunists. You just have to make sure that they're on your side.'

'I don't want them on my side.'

'They don't count, Atanas, they don't matter. They just show who's winning.'

And then, with a final push on the door, Stoyo Petkanov was gone, overnight, not allowed to pretend he was ill or making way for his successor, just packed off by the Central Committee to his house in the north-east province with a five-man guard for his own protection. At first that finger-in-the-wind deputy of his, Marinov, had tried to hold the Party together as a conservative reformist, but within weeks he was stretched and snapped on his own rack of incompatibilities. Then events began to blur like bicycle spokes; yesterday's improbable rumour became tomorrow's stale news. The Communist Party voted to suspend its leading role in the nation's political and economic development, renamed itself the Socialist Party, urged a Front for National Salvation involving all main political organisations, and when this was turned down, called for elections as soon as possible. Which the opposition parties didn't want, or at least not yet, since their structures were rudimentary and the Socialists (formerly Communists) still controlled state radio and television and most of the publishing houses and printing works, but the opposition was obliged to take its chance and won enough seats to put the Socialists (formerly Communists) on the defensive, although the Socialists (formerly Communists) still had a majority, which western commentators found incomprehensible, and the government was still inviting the opposition parties to join in and save the nation, but the opposition parties kept saying, No, *you* fucked it up, you sort it out, and if you can't sort it out, resign, and then things stumbled on with half-reforms and wrangles and insults and frustration and fear and black markets and rising prices and more half-reforms, so that none of it was heroic, or at least not in the way some had anticipated – a valiant hussar sabring through the rope of slavery – instead it was just heroic in the way that work could be heroic. Vera thought it had been like slowly prising open the fingers of a fist closed tight for half a century, a fist which held a gilded pine-cone. At last the cone fell free, badly crushed out of shape, and heavily tarnished by the sweat of years; but even in this form its weight was still the same, and its beauty just as treasured.

The last part of this process – the end of the beginning – was Petkanov's trial. So Vera insisted that the four of them be witnesses. If they couldn't get into the courtroom, they could watch the proceedings on television. Every moment of them, every minute of the nation's sudden passage from enforced adolescence to delayed maturity.

'What about the cuts?' said Atanas.

That was a problem. Every four hours – except when it was every three – there was a power cut lasting an hour – except when it lasted for two. The cuts rotated by district. Vera lived in the same electricity sector as Stefan, so that didn't help. Atanas lived a good twenty-minute bus-ride away, beyond the southern boulevards. Dimiter's district was closer, a fifteen-minute walk, an eight-minute run. So they would start at Stefan's (or Vera's when Stefan's parents got fed up with them), move to Dimiter's as first alternative, and in an emergency – if everyone else was blacked out – bus it to Atanas's.

But what if the power cut out in the middle of the trial, just as Petkanov was squirming and the prosecutor was sticking it to him, telling how he'd swindled the nation, lied and stolen, bullied and killed? They'd miss almost ten minutes' transmission running over to Dimiter's. Or worse, twenty minutes getting out to Atanas's.

'Forty,' said Atanas. What with petrol shortages and bus breakdowns, that's what you had to allow nowadays. Forty minutes!

It was Stefan, the engineer, who found the solution. Each morning the State Electricity Board published its schedule of 'interruptions', as they neutrally termed them, for the next thirty-six hours. So the plan went like this. Say they were watching at Vera's and a power cut was promised for a certain time. Two of them would set off for Dimiter's apartment ten or fifteen minutes in advance. The two left behind would watch until the picture failed, then follow the others over. At the end of the day's transmission each team would fill in the other on the ten minutes or so they had missed. Or the forty minutes, if they had to trail out beyond the southern boulevards.

'I hope they hang him,' said Dimiter the day before the trial began.

'Shoot him,' Atanas preferred. '*Takka-takka-takka-takka.*'

'I hope we learn the truth,' said Vera.

'I hope they just let him talk,' said Stefan. 'Just ask him simple questions to which there are simple answers, and then hear him come out with all that shit. How much did you steal? When did you order the murder of Simeon Popov? What is the number of your Swiss bank account? Ask him things like that, and watch how he doesn't answer a single one of them.'

'I want to see film of his palaces,' said Dimiter. 'And pictures of all his mistresses.'

'We don't know he had mistresses,' said Vera. 'Anyway, that's not important.'

'I want to know exactly how dangerous our nuclear plants are,' said Stefan.

'I want to know if he personally authorised the Department of External Security to try and kill the Pope,' said Dimiter.

'I want to see him shot,' said Atanas.

'I want to know about the Politburo's privileges,' said Dimiter.

'I want to know how much we owe, each of us,' said Stefan.

'*Takka-takka-takka,*' went Atanas. '*Takka-takka-takka.*'

\*

The week before Criminal Law Case Number 1 opened in the Supreme Court, former President Stoyo Petkanov sent an open letter to the National Assembly. He intended to promote his own defence vigorously, both to the people and to the parliament, on television and in the press, until such time as the fascist tendencies currently at work succeeded in gagging him. The text of his letter ran as follows:

Esteemed National Representatives,
Certain circumstances compel me to address this letter to you. These circumstances lead me to believe that certain people want to turn me into a means of achieving their own political interests and personal ambitions. I would like to declare that I will not play into the hands of any political group.

As far as I know, a single head of state has been tried and convicted in modern history so far: Emperor Bokassa in Africa (who was convicted) for conspiracy, murders and cannibalism. I will be the second case.

24

As to my personal responsibility, I can tell you even now, fully aware and having summed my life up after long contemplation, that as this country's party leader and head of state for 33 years I bear the greatest political responsibility for everything done. Did the good things outnumber the bad things, did we live in darkness and hopelessness during all those years, did mothers give birth to children, were we calm or anxious, did the people have any goals and ideals: I have no right to judge all this myself now.

The answers to all these questions can only come from our own people and our history. I am sure that they will be stern judges. I am convinced, however, that they will be fair too, categorically rejecting both political nihilism and total denigration.

I have done everything in the belief that it was good for my country. I have made mistakes along the way, but I have not committed crimes against my people. It is for these mistakes that I accept political responsibility.

3rd January

Respectfully yours,
Stoyo Petkanov

*

Like most of his contemporaries, Peter Solinsky had grown up within the Party. A Red Pioneer, a Young Socialist, and then a full party member, he had received his card shortly before his father fell victim to one of Petkanov's routine purges and was exiled to the country. There had been sour words between them at first, since Peter, with all the

authority of youth, knew that the Party was always greater than the individual, and that this applied in his father's
case as in anyone else's. Peter himself had naturally fallen
under suspicion for a while; and he acknowledged in those
clouded days that marriage to the daughter of a hero in the
Anti-Fascist Struggle had given him some protection. Slowly,
he had regained favour with the Party; once, they had even
sent him to Turin as part of a trade delegation. They had
issued him with foreign currency and told him to spend it;
he had felt privileged. Maria, understandably, had not been
permitted to accompany him.

At forty, he had been appointed professor of law at the
capital's second university. The apartment in Friendship 3
had then seemed luxurious; they owned a small car and a
cottage in the Ostova woods; they had limited but regular
access to the Special Shops. Angelina, their daughter, was
cheerful, spoiled, and happy at being spoiled. What made
these solutions to life insufficient? What had turned him
– as *Truth* had put it only that morning – into a political
parricide?

Looking back, he supposed that it had started with Angelina, with her *whys*. Not the confident, ritualistic *whys* of a
four-year-old (why is it Sunday? why are we going? why is it
a taxi?) but the considered, tentative *whys* of a child of ten.
Why were there so many soldiers when there wasn't a war?
Why were there so many apricot trees in the countryside
but never apricots in the shops? Why is there fog over the
city in the summer? Why do all those people live on that
waste ground beyond the eastern boulevards? The questions
were not dangerous, and Peter had answered easily enough.
Because they are there to protect us. Because we sell them
abroad for hard currency that we need. Because there are

many factories working at full capacity. Because gypsies choose to live that way.

Angelina was always content with the answers. That was the shock. He hadn't been a father prodded into doubt by an innocent child's potent questions; what stirred him was the innocent child's passive satisfaction with responses he knew to be at best plausible evasions. Her blithe acceptance troubled him profoundly. As he lay awake, fretting in the dark, Angelina's condition expanded until it became symptomatic of the whole country. Could a nation lose its capacity for scepticism, for useful doubt? What if the muscle of contradiction simply atrophied from lack of exercise?

A year or so later, Peter Solinsky discovered that such fears were over-pessimistic. Sceptics and oppositionists were tactically quiet in his presence because they were roundly suspicious of him. But people did exist who wanted to try again from the beginning, who preferred facts to ideology, who wanted to establish small truths before proceeding to the larger ones. When Peter realised that there were enough such people to encourage the timid majority to stir, he felt as if the smog was lifting from his soul.

It had all begun in a medium-sized town on the northern border with their nearest socialist ally. A river ran between the two states here, a river from which no fish had been taken for years. The trees above the town grew twisted and low, rarely putting out leaves. Prevailing winds blew a greasy, dun-coloured air across the river from another medium-sized town on the southern border of the nearest socialist ally. Children developed chest ailments from infancy; women wrapped scarves round their faces before going out to shop; doctors' surgeries were full of burnt lungs and tortured eyes. Until one day a group of women sent a protest to the capital. And since by chance the nearest socialist ally was passingly in disfavour for being less than fraternal towards one of its ethnic minorities, the letter to the Minister of Health turned into a small paragraph in *Truth*, which the next day was alluded to sympathetically by a member of the Politburo.

So a small protest became a local movement and then a Green Party, which was permitted to exist as a sop to Gorbachev while severely instructed to concern itself with nothing but environmental matters, and preferably those which might embarrass the nearest socialist ally. Whereupon three hundred thousand people joined the new movement and started tugging at the nettle-roots of political cause and effect: from regional secretary to provincial secretary to Central Committee Department to deputy minister to minister to Politburo to presidential whim; from dead tree to living five-year plan. By the time the Central Committee realised the danger and declared membership of the Greens incompatible with Socialism and Communism, Peter Solinsky and thousands like him cared far more about their new party card than their old one. It was too late then for a purge; too late to stop Ilia Banov, that slyly telegenic ex-Communist turned leader of the Greens, from grabbing national popularity; too late to avoid the elections forced upon the socialist countries by Gorbachev; too late, as Stoyo Petkanov told the eleven-man Politburo in emergency session, to prevent the whole fucking lid from blowing off.

Maria Solinska's private opinion – and increasingly her opinions tended to be private – was that the Green Party was a collection of cretinous foresters, hooligan anarchists, and fascist sympathisers; that Ilia Banov should have been put on a flight to Franco's Spain thirty years ago; and that her husband Peter, having striven for so long to obtain a good job and a decent apartment, having avoided the malign shadow of his deviationist father largely thanks to her presence, was either losing whatever small political sense he once had, or else suffering a mid-life crisis, and quite possibly both at the same time.

She kept quiet while some she knew reviled the beliefs they had loyally upheld a few months earlier; she observed the furious glee of the crowds, and on every boulevard of the city she smelt revenge like sour sweat. She withdrew increasingly into her life with Angelina. At times she envied the child learning simple, certain things like mathematics and music, and wished she could join her. But then she would also have had to learn the new political certainties, the new orthodoxies they rushed to teach at school.

Nevertheless, on the first morning of Criminal Law Case Number 1, when her husband came to kiss her goodbye, something stirred within her, and made her forget the quick betrayals and slow disappointments of the last few years. So Maria Solinska kissed Peter back, and with an affectionate fussiness she had not displayed for some time, straightened the scarf-ends he had jammed hastily between his turned-out lapels. 'Be careful,' she said as he left.

'Careful? Of course I shall be careful. Look,' he said, putting down his briefcase and holding up his hands, 'I am wearing my porcupine gloves.'

\*

Criminal Law Case Number 1 began in the Supreme Court on the 10th of January. The former President was seen arriving under military escort: a short, stout figure in a buttoned-up

29

mackintosh. He wore his familiar heavy glasses with a slight tint in the lens, and when he got out of the Chaika he took off his hat, letting viewers see yet again the head familiar from so many of the nation's postage stamps: the skull set low on the shoulders, the sharp, questing nose, the frontal baldness and the stiff, sandy-coloured hair over his ears. There was a crowd, and so he smiled and waved. Then the camera lost sight of him until he re-emerged into the courtroom. Somewhere along the burrow he had left his hat and coat: now there was a sombre, square-cut suit, a white shirt and a green tie striped diagonally with grey. He stopped and looked around, like a footballer surveying an unfamiliar stadium. Just as he seemed about to move forward, he changed his mind and stepped across to one of the soldiers on guard. He peered at a medal ribbon, and then, almost as an afterthought, paternally adjusted the militiaman's tunic. He smiled to himself, and walked on.

['*Such a fucking ham.*'
'*Shh, Atanas.*']

The courtroom had been built in an early-Seventies' mode of softened brutalism: pale wood, flattened angles, chairs that approached comfort. It could have been a rehearsal theatre, or a small concert hall in which spiky wind quintets were played, except for the lighting, a drab collaboration of strip neon and cowled down-lamps. It gave no favouritism or focus; the effect was flat, democratic, unjudging.

Petkanov was shown to the dock, where he stood for a few moments, looking round at the two rows of lawyers' desks, the small public gallery, the raised bench where the President of the Court and his two assessors would sit; he scrutinised the guards, the ushers, the television cameras, the push of pressmen. There were so many journalists that some had to be accommodated in the jury box, where a sudden self-consciousness hit them: thoughtfully, they began examining their empty notebooks.

Eventually, the former President sat down on the small hard chair that had been chosen for him. Behind, and therefore always in shot when Petkanov was on camera, stood an ordinary prison officer. The prosecution had arranged this little touch of stage management, and suggested in particular that a woman guard be chosen. The military were to be kept out of the picture as far as possible. See, this is just another civilian case in which a criminal is brought to justice; and look, he is no longer the monster who terrified us, he is just an old man guarded by women.

The President of the Court and his colleagues entered: three elderly men in dark suits, white shirts and black ties, the most senior of them identifiable by a loose black gown. The trial was declared open, and the Prosecutor General invited to read the charges. Peter Solinsky, already on his feet, looked across at Stoyo Petkanov, waiting for him to stand up. But the former President remained where he was, head slightly on one side, a powerful man comfortably seated in the royal box, waiting for the curtain to rise. The wardress leaned forward and whispered something, which he pretended not to hear.

Solinsky did not react to this studied contrariness. Quietly, ordinarily, he went about his work. First he took as long and deep a breath as was possible without anyone noticing. Control of the lungs, he had been taught, was the key to advocacy. Only athletes, opera singers and lawyers understood the importance of how you breathed.

[*'Stick it up his arse, Solinsky, go on, stick it up his arse.'*
*'Shh.'*]

'Stoyo Petkanov, you are charged before the Supreme Court of this nation with the following offences. First, deception involving documents, under Article 127 (3) of the Penal Code. Second, abuse of authority in your official capacity, under Article 212 (4) of the Penal Code. And thirdly . . .

[*'Mass murder.'*

*'Genocide.'*

*'Ruining the country.'*]

. . . mismanagement under Article 332 (8) of the Penal Code.'

[*'Mismanagement!'*

*'Mismanagement of the prison camps.'*

*'He didn't torture people properly enough.'*

*'Shit. Shit.'*]

'How do you plead?'

Petkanov remained in exactly the same position, only now with a faint smile on his face. The wardress leaned towards him again, but he stopped her with a flick of the fingers.

Solinsky turned for help to the President of the Court, who said, 'The accused will answer the question. How do you plead?'

Petkanov merely cocked his head a little more, delivering the same wanly supercilious expression to the judicial bench.

The President of the Court looked across to the defence counsel. State Advocate Milanova, a dark, severe woman in early middle age, was already on her feet. 'The defence has been instructed not to enter a plea,' she announced.

The three judges conferred briefly, then their President announced, 'Silence is interpreted by the court as a plea of not guilty under Article 465. Continue.'

Solinsky began again. 'You are Stoyo Petkanov?'

The former President seemed to be considering the question for a few moments. Then, with a slight cough, as if making clear that the movement which followed came from his own volition, he stood up. But still he made no attempt to speak. The Prosecutor General therefore repeated, 'You are Stoyo Petkanov?'

The accused took no notice of the prosecutor in his shiny Italian suit, and turned instead to the President of the Court. 'I wish to make an opening statement.'

'First answer the Prosecutor General's question.'

The Second Leader looked back at Solinsky as if noticing him for the first time, and inviting him to repeat his question like a schoolboy.

'You are Stoyo Petkanov?'

'You know I am. I fought with your father against the Fascists. I sent you to Italy to buy your suit. I approved your appointment as professor of law. You know very well who I am. I wish to make a statement.'

'If it is brief,' replied the President of the Court.

Petkanov nodded to himself, taking in and yet ignoring the judge's request. He looked around the courtroom as if he had only just become aware of the place, settled his spectacles a little higher up his nose, laid his fists on the padded wooden bar in front of him, and asked, in the tone of one used to better organisation of a public event, 'Which camera am I on?'

['*The shit, listen to him, the bastard.*'
'*We don't buy it, Stoyo, we don't buy it any more.*'
'*I hope he dies in front of us. Live on TV.*'
'*Calm down, Atanas. You'll croak if you go on like that.*']
'Make your statement.'

33

Petkanov nodded again, more in self-consultation than acknowledgement of another's instructions. 'I do not recognise the authority of this court. It does not have the power to try me. I was illegally arrested, illegally imprisoned, illegally interrogated and am now before a court which is illegally constituted. However . . . ' and here he allowed himself a pause, and a quick smile, knowing that his 'However' had cut off an interruption from the bench, ' . . . However, I will answer your questions provided they are relevant.'

He paused again, allowing the Prosecutor General time to wonder if that was the end of his statement or not. 'And I will answer your questions for a simple reason. I have been here before. Not in this very courtroom, true. But more than fifty years ago, long before I became helmsman to the nation. With other comrades I was helping organise the Anti-Fascist Struggle in Velpen. We were protesting against the imprisonment of railway workers. It was a peaceful democratic protest but of course it was attacked by the bourgeois-landlord police. I was beaten up, so were all the comrades. In prison we discussed how we were to proceed. Some of the comrades argued that we should refuse to answer the court on the grounds that we had been illegally arrested and illegally imprisoned and that the evidence against us was being fabricated by the police. But I convinced them that it was more vital to warn the nation about the dangers of Fascism and the preparations for war by the imperialist powers. And that is what we did. As you know, we were sentenced to hard labour for our defence of the proletariat.

'And now,' he went on, 'I look around this court and I am not surprised. I have been here before. And therefore, once again, I consent to answer your questions, provided they are relevant.'

'You are Stoyo Petkanov?' the prosecutor repeated, with an emphatic weariness, as if it were not his fault that justice required him to pose every question in quadruplicate.

'Yes, indeed, we have established that.'

'Then, being Stoyo Petkanov, you will know that your conviction by the court in Velpen on 21st October 1935 was for criminal damage to property, theft of an iron railing, and criminal assault with the said stolen item on a member of the national police.'

When the camera cut back to Petkanov, *Atanas took a deep puff of his cigarette and exhaled through narrow, pushed-out lips. The smoke hit the screen and flattened against it, drifting away. It was better than spitting, thought Atanas. I spit in your face with smoke.*

\*

Peter Solinsky had not been first choice for the post of prosecutor general. His experience was largely academic, and only partly in criminal law. But he knew after his first interview that he had done well. Other, more qualified candidates had played politics, suggested conditions; some, after consulting their families, had discovered previous commitments. But Solinsky had manifestly wanted the job; he came with specific ideas about the framing of charges; and he boldly proposed that his own years of party membership might even be an advantage in trying to ensnare Petkanov. Set a fox to catch a wolf, he had quoted, and the minister had smiled. In this slim, anxious-eyed professor he identified a pragmatism and an aggression which he thought necessary in a prosecutor general.

The appointment came as little surprise to Peter. His

life, when he examined it, seemed to consist of long periods of caution followed by moments of decisiveness, even recklessness, in which he got what he wanted. He had been a dutiful child, a good student; obedience to his parents' wishes even led him to get engaged on his twentieth birthday to their neighbours' daughter Pavlina. Three months later he had jilted her for Maria, and insisted on marrying at once, with so much sudden obstinate zeal that his parents had naturally examined the girl's belly. They were puzzled when the next months did not bear out their suspicions.

After that, for many years, he had been a loyal party member and good husband – or was it a good party member and loyal husband? Sometimes the two conditions seemed muddlingly close in his mind. Then, one evening, he announced that he had joined the Green Party at a time when, as Maria vigorously pointed out, it contained very few professors of law married to the daughters of anti-fascist heroes. Worse, Peter had not simply gone along to a few meetings on the sly; he had sent back his party card with an openly provocative letter which a few years earlier would have brought men in leather coats to the door at an unsocial hour.

Now, according to his wife, he was indulging his vanity again. His colleagues simply judged his appointment an enviable career move, one revealing in the courteous and enclosed lawyer a secret wish for television stardom. But then such people saw only Solinsky's outer life, and tended to assume that his inner existence must be equally well ordered. In fact, he oscillated constantly between different levels of anxiety, and his intermittent thrusts of decisiveness were intended to allay the fret and stew within him. If nations can behave like individuals, he was an

36

individual who behaved like a nation: enduring decades of edgy submissiveness, then bursting into revolt, eager for fresh rhetoric and a renewed image of himself.

In prosecuting the former Head of State, Peter Solinsky was embarking on his most public form of self-definition. To newspaper columnists and TV commentators he represented the new order against the old, the future against the past, virtue against vice; and when he spoke to the media he customarily invoked the national conscience, moral duty, his plan of easing truth like a dandelion leaf from between the teeth of lies. But in the background lay feelings he did not care to inspect very closely. They were to do with cleanliness, personal rather than symbolic; with the knowledge that his father was dying; and with the desire to force upon himself a maturity which mere time was failing to supply.

The post of prosecutor general had only become available after extensive public debate. Many had argued against a trial. Surely it was better for the nation to let bygones be bygones, and focus its energy on reconstruction? This would also be more prudent, as no-one could claim that Petkanov was the only guilty person in the country. How far through the nomenklatura, the Party, the security police, the regular police, the civilian informers, the magistracy and the military was guilt held to run? If there was to be justice, some argued, then it should be full justice, a proper accounting, since the select punishment of a few, let alone a single individual, was obvious injustice. Yet how far was 'full justice' distinguishable from mere revenge?

Others pressed for what they called a 'moral trial', but as no nation in the history of the world had ever held one before, it was unclear what the thing might consist of, or what sort of evidence might be adduced. Besides, who had the right to judge, and did not the assertion of that right imply a sinister self-elevation? Surely God was the only person capable of presiding over a moral trial. Terrestrials were better off concerning themselves with who stole what from whom.

All solutions were flawed, but the most flawed was to do nothing, and to do nothing slowly. They must do something quickly. A Special Parliamentary Committee therefore appointed a Special Investigatory Office with the understanding that while all its enquiries were to be conducted with an even greater diligence and thoroughness than usual, the case against Stoyo Petkanov must be ready to start by early January. It was also stressed that correct juridical procedures must be followed. The days were gone of laying a broad charge which could then be interpreted by the court as covering whatever behaviour the State decided to punish. The Special Investigatory Office was instructed to establish exactly what Petkanov had done that infringed his own laws, to assemble trustworthy evidence, and then decide the charges. This involved a considerable reversal of traditional thinking.

The Special Office found straightforward proof of malpractice hard to obtain. Little was written down; what had been written down was mostly destroyed; and those who had destroyed it suffered reliable attacks of memory loss. A wider problem came from the unitary nature of the State which had just collapsed. Article 1 of the New Constitution of 1971 had enacted the leading role of the Party. From that moment Party and State merged into one, and any clear separation between a political organisation and a legislative system ceased to exist. What was judged politically necessary was, by definition, legal.

38

Eventually, under increasing pressure, the Special Office discovered enough evidence to recommend proceeding with three charges. The first, deception involving documents, related to the receipt of undue royalties from the former President's writings and speeches. The second, abuse of authority committed in an official capacity, covered a wide range of benefits allegedly given and received by the former President, and was helpful in demonstrating the extent of corruption under the communist system. The third, mismanagement, concerned a payment of undue social benefit to the former Chairman of the Environmental Protection Committee. The Special Office was rather embarrassed by this, since the other person named was a marginal figure now in frail health; but it was agreed that a mere two charges were insufficient for such a historic indictment. The Special Office also recommended that as the circumstances of the case were exceptional, the prosecution be allowed to present newly discovered evidence in mid-trial, and to add further charges if necessary as the case proceeded. Despite much criticism, these provisions were adopted.

*

Since Petkanov declined to co-operate with State Defence Advocates Milanova and Zlatarova, it was decided that the normal professional courtesies between prosecution and defence would have to be extended to the accused in person. Accordingly, when the court adjourned, Peter Solinsky went to the sixth floor of the Ministry of Justice (formerly Office of State Security), taking with him documents which the defence had a right to see. In these second encounters of the day the former President was often more relaxed, but not necessarily more agreeable.

Each morning a militiaman brought Stoyo Petkanov the five national newspapers and laid them on his table in a pile. Each morning Petkanov extracted *Truth*, the mouthpiece of the Socialist (formerly Communist) Party, and left untouched *The Nation*, *The People*, *Liberty* and *Free Times*.

'You are not interested in what the devil has to say?' Solinsky asked lightly one afternoon, when he found Petkanov hunched over party gospel.

'The devil?'

'The journalists of our free press.'

'Free, *free*. You make such a fetish of that word. Does it make your prick swell? Freedom, freedom, let's see your pants stir, Solinsky.'

'You're not in court now. There's no-one watching.' Only a militiaman acting the deaf-mute.

'Freedom,' said Petkanov with emphasis, 'freedom consists in conforming to the will of the majority.'

Solinsky did not respond at first. He had heard that line before and it terrified him. Finally he murmured, 'You really believe that?'

'Everything else you call freedom is merely the privilege of a social élite.'

'Like the Special Shops for party members? Did they conform to the will of the majority?'

Petkanov threw down the newspaper. 'Journalists are whores. I prefer my own whores.'

The Prosecutor General found these exchanges frustrating but useful. He needed to learn his opponent, to feel him, to discover how to predict his unpredictabilities. So he continued, in a pedantically reasonable tone, 'There are differences of category, you know. Perhaps you should read *Free Times* on your trial. It does not take the obvious position.'

'I could spare myself the trouble and pour a bucket of shit over my head instead.'

'You don't want to understand, do you?'

'Solinsky, you have no idea how this discussion wearies me. We considered all this decades ago and came to the correct conclusions. Even your father agreed, after spinning like a top for several months. You have given him my warm greetings?'

'The term "free newspaper" doesn't mean anything to you, does it?'

Petkanov sighed melodramatically, as if the Prosecutor General were arguing flat-earth theory. 'It's a contradiction. All newspapers belong to some party, some interest. Either the capitalists or the people. I'm surprised you haven't noticed.'

'There are newspapers which are owned by the journalists who write them.'

'Then the party they represent is the worst of all, the party of egoism. A pure expression of bourgeois individualism.'

'And there are even journalists, it may surprise you to learn, who change their opinions on subjects. Who have the freedom to come to their own conclusions, then to examine them, to re-examine them, and alter their views.'

'Unreliable whores, you mean,' said Petkanov. 'Neurotic whores.'

*

There had been a Revolution, of that there was no doubt; but the word was never used, not even in a qualified form, preceded by Velvet or Gentle. This country had the fullest sense of history, but also a great wariness of rhetoric. The high expectations of the last years refused to declare themselves in tall words. So instead of Revolution, people here spoke only of the Changes, and history was now divided into three quiet parts: before the Changes, during the Changes, after the Changes. Look what had happened throughout history: Reformation, Counter-Reformation, Revolution, Counter-Revolution, Fascism, Anti-Fascism, Communism, Anti-Communism. Great movements, as by some law of physics, seemed to provoke an equal and opposite force. So people talked cautiously of the Changes, and this slight evasion made them feel a little safer: it was difficult to imagine something called the Counter-Changes or the Anti-Changes, and therefore such a reality might be avoidable too.

Meanwhile, slowly, discreetly, the monuments were coming down all over the city. There had been partial removals before, of course. One year, bronze Stalins had been purged at a whisper from Moscow. They had been taken from their plinths in the night and delivered to a patch of waste ground near the central marshalling yard, where they were lined up against a high wall as if awaiting the firing squad. For a few weeks two militiamen had guarded them, until it became clear that there was little popular desire to desecrate these effigies. So they were surrounded with barbed wire and left to fend for themselves, kept awake through the night by the hoot and moan of goods trains. Each spring the nettles grew a little higher, and bindweed made a fresh curling run up the inside leg of the booted war-leader. Occasionally an intruder with hammer and chisel would climb one of

42

the shorter monuments and attempt to chip off a souvenir half-moustache; but drink or the inadequacy of the chisel always brought failure. The statues lingered on beside the marshalling yard, shiny in the rain and as undefeated as a memory.

Now Stalin had company. Brezhnev, who favoured bronze and granite postures in life, and now happily continued his existence as a statue. Lenin, with worker's cap and inspiringly raised arm, the fingers clasping holy writ. Next to him the nation's First Leader, who in a permanent gesture of political subservience loyally remained a metre or so shorter than the giants of Soviet Russia. And now came Stoyo Petkanov, displaying himself in various guises: as partisan leader with pigskin sandals and peasant's blouse; as military commander with Stalinist knee-boots and general's ribbons; as world statesman with boxy, double-breasted suit and Order of Lenin in the buttonhole. This close, select company, some of its later representatives roughly mutilated by an unsympathetic crane, huddled together in permanent exile, silently discussing policy.

Recently, there was talk of Alyosha joining them. Alyosha, who had stood on that low northern hill for almost four decades, his bayonet glittering fraternally. He had been a gift from the Soviet people; now there was a movement to return him to his donors. Let him go back to Kiev or Kalinin or wherever: he must be getting homesick after all this time, and his great bronze mother must be missing him badly.

But symbolic gestures can prove expensive. It had been cheap enough to sneak the embalmed First Leader out of his Mausoleum on a forgotten night when only one street-lamp in six was lit. But repatriating Alyosha? That would cost thousands of American dollars, money better spent on buying oil or mending the leaky nuclear reactor in the eastern province. So some argued instead for a gentler, local banishment. Pack him off to the marshalling yard and let him join his metallic masters. He would tower over them there, for he was the largest statue in the country; and that might be a small, inexpensive revenge, the thought of those vain leaders discountenanced by his huge arrival.

Others believed that Alyosha should stay on his hill. It was, after all, indisputably true that the Soviet army had liberated the country from the Fascists, and that Russian soldiers had died and been buried here; true also that at the time, and for a while afterwards, many had been grateful to Alyosha and his comrades. Why not let him remain where he was? You did not have to agree with every monument. You did not destroy the Pyramids in retrospective guilt at the sufferings of the Egyptian slaves.

*

At nine thirty one morning, Peter Solinsky was standing beside his office desk, soundlessly interrogating one corner of the bookcase fifteen feet away. This was how he practised for the day's work. He was midway through a question which stretched the legal rules a little, being less an enquiry than a factual hypothesis with implicit moral denunciation, when the telephone irritatingly announced a visitor. Solinsky briefly excused the bookcase, which was perspiring and mopping its brow in a guilty fashion, and directed his attention to Georgi Ganin, Head of the Patriotic Security Forces (formerly the Department of Internal Security).

Nowadays Ganin wore a suit, to indicate that his work

was an unthreatening, civilian business. But on that day, only a couple of years ago, when he had come to fortunate fame, his corpulence had been trussed up in a lieutenant's uniform, and his shoulder-flashes pronounced him a member of the North-West Provincial Military Command. He had been sent with twenty militiamen to control what had confidently been described as an unimportant demonstration in the regional capital of Sliven.

It was indeed a small gathering: three hundred local Greens and oppositionists in a sloping cobbled square, stamping their feet and clapping their hands as much to keep warm as anything else. In front of the Communist Party headquarters rose a fat barricade of dirty snow, which in itself would normally have been sufficient protection. But two factors made the occasion different. The first was the presence of the Devinsky Commando, a student organisation which had not yet qualified for a security file. This was hardly surprising, since information on student behaviour had lately become difficult to obtain; and in any case, the Devinsky Commando was registered as a literary society, named after Ivan Devinsky, poet of the region, who despite various decadent and formalist tendencies had proved a patriot and martyr during the fascist invasion of 1941. The second factor was the chance attendance of a Swedish TV team whose locally hired car had broken down the previous day, and who now found themselves with nothing to film but a piece of routine provincial dissent.

Had the security police investigated the Devinsky Commando, they might have discovered that the poet had a reputation as an ironist and provocateur; and that in 1929 his 'loyal sonnet' entitled 'Thank You, Your Majesty' had led immediately to a three-year exile in Paris. The members

45

of the student Commando identified themselves by wearing the red bonnets of Junior Pioneers: headgear for ten-year-olds, which was either ludicrously stretched or else satirically attached to the crown with a girlfriend's hair-clip. The other protesters, like the security forces, had never heard of the Devinsky Commando, and were irritated by what looked like a group of pro-communist infiltrators. Their suspicions were confirmed when the Devinskyites unfurled a banner reading WE, LOYAL STUDENTS, WORKERS AND PEASANTS, SUPPORT THE GOVERNMENT.

Pushing their way to the front of the demonstration, the Commando took up a position close to the bank of dirty snow and began to chant. 'LONG LIVE THE PARTY. LONG LIVE THE GOVERNMENT. LONG LIVE THE PARTY. LONG LIVE THE GOVERNMENT. ALL HONOUR TO STOYO PETKANOV. LONG LIVE THE PARTY.'

After a couple of minutes, the tall french windows on the reviewing balcony opened, and the local party chief emerged to witness for himself a display of support rare in these counter-revolutionary days. Immediately the students widened their repertoire of chants. With fists patriotically raised and red bonnets forming a loyal phalanx, they acclaimed the smiling boss of Sliven:

'THANK YOU FOR THE PRICE RISES.'

'THANK YOU FOR THE FOOD SHORTAGES.'

'GIVE US IDEOLOGY NOT BREAD.'

The students were well drilled and had loud voices. Their fists punched the air, and there was no hesitation as they switched from one slogan to another.

'THANK YOU FOR THE PRICE RISES.'

'STRENGTHEN THE SECURITY POLICE.'

'LONG LIVE THE PARTY.'

'HONOUR TO STOYO PETKANOV.'

'THANK YOU FOR THE FOOD SHORTAGES.'

'GIVE US IDEOLOGY NOT BREAD.'

Suddenly, as if they had taken a silent vote, the rest of the crowd joined in. 'THANK YOU FOR THE FOOD SHORT-AGES' began to echo furiously round the square, the party chief banged shut the french windows, and the demonstration suddenly acquired a hysterical edge which Ganin knew to be dangerous. His men were drawn up at the side of the building, and they now caught the attention of the Devinsky Commando. Three times the platoon of students advanced a few dozen metres towards the militiamen, chanting:

'THANK YOU FOR THE BULLETS.'

'THANK YOU FOR THE MARTYRDOM.'

'THANK YOU FOR THE BULLETS.'

'THANK YOU FOR THE MARTYRDOM.'

It was noticeable that the Greens and oppositionists preferred not to take up this cry, waiting for the Commando to rejoin them before calling once more in favour of price rises and food shortages. The TV crew were by this time in position and filming.

Ganin received the order from a stranger in a leather coat, who emerged swiftly from a side door of the party headquarters, mentioned a name and security rank, and instructed him, as a direct order from the party chief, to fire over the heads of the demonstrators, and if that did not disperse them, to fire at their feet. His message imparted, the man disappeared back into the building, though not before his presence had been noted by the students.

'PLEASE MAY WE JOIN THE SECURITY FORCES,' they bellowed, then, 'THANK YOU FOR THE BULLETS. PLEASE MAY WE JOIN THE SECURITY FORCES.'

Ganin marched his men forward twenty metres. The Commando came to meet them. Ganin tried to look confident as he gave the order to aim over the heads of the crowd, but several things alarmed him. First, the authority of the instructions he had received. Second, the fear that some idiot ranker would decide to lower his aim. And third, the knowledge that each militiaman had only one clip of bullets. THANK YOU FOR THE SHORTAGES was a cry which had its echo in the army too.

With a delaying hand raised to his troops, Ganin walked towards the Commando. At the same time a young man wearing two Junior Pioneer bonnets, one clipped over each ear, detached himself from the students. Swedish Television caught the decisive meeting of these two, the bearded student in big red ear-mufflers, and the rotund, pink-cheeked army officer, his breath fogging out before him in the cold air. The cameraman bravely moved in closer, but the sound recordist had sudden thoughts of his family back in Karlstad. This moment of prudence was just as well for the young lieutenant. Had the ensuing conversation been preserved, his rise to authority might have been slower.

'So, Comrade Officer, are you going to kill us all?'

'Just go. Disperse and we will not shoot.'

'But we like it here. We have no classes at the moment. We were enjoying our exchange of views with Party Chief Krumov. Perhaps you could ask the loyal security officer why his esteemed boss broke off our productive discussions.'

Ganin had to make an effort not to smile. 'I order you to disperse.'

But the student, instead of obeying, came even closer, linking his arm with the lieutenant's. 'So, Comrade Officer, how many of us have you been ordered to kill? Twenty? Thirty? All of us?'

'Frankly,' replied Ganin, 'that's not possible. We don't have enough bullets. What with the shortages.'

The student burst out laughing and kissed Ganin suddenly on both cheeks. The pink-faced lieutenant laughed back, his face filling the eye-piece of the Swedish cameraman. 'Look,' he said confidentially, 'I'm sure we can work something out.'

'Of course we can, Comrade Officer.' He turned away, and shouted back to his colleagues, 'MORE BULLETS FOR THE SOLDIERS.'

As the Devinsky Commando advanced, their red bonnets flopping, with alternate cries of DOWN WITH THE SHORTAGES and MORE BULLETS FOR THE SOLDIERS, Ganin gestured uneasily at his men to lower their rifles. They did so anxiously, and didn't look much happier when each of the students picked out a soldier and embraced him vigorously. But the pictures were splendidly dramatic, and the lack of sound enabled viewers to imagine dialogue which was inevitably more noble. Ganin was transformed in this moment from an indecisive, if not cowardly, junior officer into a symbol of decency, an advertisement for the power of negotiation and the middle way; while his brief, silent exchange of pluming breaths in a cobbled square before a palisade of dirty snow was widely taken as a sign that the army, if forced to choose between the people and the Party, would place its support behind the people.

Thereafter, Ganin's rise had been so swift that his wife Nina scarcely had time to tack a new rank on his uniform before it became outdated. She was pleased when he moved into civilian clothes; but her amused relief was premature. The dinners Georgi found himself obliged to attend meant that regular alterations had to be made to his suits as well. Now he stood in Solinsky's office, a corpulent civil servant, red-faced from climbing the stairs, his middle button under pressure despite the doubled thread Nina had used. Awkwardly, he offered a cardboard file to the Prosecutor General.

'Tell me about it,' said Solinsky.

'Comrade Prosecutor . . . '

'Mr Prosecutor will do,' Solinsky smiled. 'Lieutenant-General.'

'Mr Prosecutor, sir. We in the Patriotic Security Forces wish to encourage you in your work and trust that your diligence will be rewarded.'

Solinsky smiled again. It would take a while for the old forms of address to die away. 'What is in the folder?'

'We trust that the accused will be found guilty on all charges.'

'Yes, yes.'

'Such a verdict would be greatly helpful to the PSF in their current restructuring.'

'Well, that's a matter for the court.'

'And a matter of evidence.'

'General . . . '

'Of course, sir. This is a preliminary report on the case of Anna Petkanova. The core files have unfortunately been destroyed.'

'Hardly surprising.'

'No, sir. But even though the core files were destroyed much has been patriotically saved. Even if access and identification are not always easy.'

' . . . ?'

'Yes. As you will see, there is preliminary evidence of

50

the involvement of the Department of Internal Security in the case of Anna Petkanova.'

Solinsky was barely interested. 'There are dead pigs under every hedge,' he replied. Frankly, there was little in the public life of the nation over the last fifty years which, on examination, would not disclose preliminary evidence of the involvement of the Department of Internal Security.

'Yes, sir.' Ganin was still holding out the folder. 'You wish us to keep you informed?'

'If . . . ' Solinsky accepted the file almost absent-mindedly. 'If you think it appropriate.' Hmmm. How easily he fell back on the old formulas. *If you think it appropriate*. And why had he said *There are dead pigs under every hedge*? That wasn't the way he talked. It sounded like the defendant in Criminal Law Case Number 1. Perhaps he was being infected. He must practise saying *Yes* and *No* and *That's stupid* and *Go away*.

'We wish you good fortune with the continuation of the prosecution, Mr Prosecutor, sir.'

'Yes, thank you.' Go away. Put a soldier into civvies and the length of his sentences doubled. 'Thank you.' Go away.

*

Vera crossed the Square of St Vassily the Martyr, which had, in the course of the last forty years, also been Stalingrad Square, Brezhnev Square, and even, briefly, in an attempt to get round the whole problem, the Square of the Heroes of Socialism. For several months now it had lapsed into anonymity. Bare, stumpy metal posts imitated the dormant chestnut trees. Both were waiting for spring:

the trees to get back their leaves and the posts to sprout name-plates. Then the city would once again have a Square of St Vassily the Martyr.

Vera knew she was pretty. She was pleased with her high cheekbones and wide-set brown eyes, approved her legs, felt that the bright colours she wore suited her. But crossing the public gardens in the Square of St Vassily, as she did each morning at ten o'clock, mysteriously turned her into a frump. This had been happening now for months. There were up to a hundred men clustered by the garden's western gate, and not a single one of them looked at her. Or if they did, they looked away at once, not even bothering to check her legs, not smiling at the chiffon burst around her neck.

Before the Changes, any public gathering of more than eight people had to be officially registered, and the registration procedure might be very *ad hoc*, consisting of men in leather coats demanding to know names and addresses. Since the Changes, sights like this, of a loosely swirling vortex of people, had become common. Some passers-by joined in automatically, as they would attach themselves to any queue outside a shop in the theoretical hope of a few eggs or half a kilo of carrots. The odd thing about the crowd here was that it consisted entirely of men, most between the ages of eighteen and thirty: in other words, the sort of men who *always* looked at her. But instead they were in a state of ordered excitement, as one by one, in a scarcely observable, apian process, they were sucked from the outer fringe of the group to the middle, and then, after a few minutes, expelled. Some seemed to have got what they wanted, and headed purposefully through the western gates; the rest drifted off aimlessly in any direction.

Pornography, that was Vera's first explanation. You

saw groups of men gathered heatedly around an upturned beer-crate on which some badly printed magazine was being displayed. Or sometimes what stood there was a bottle of foreign spirits and a few small glasses; the bottle normally came from the waste-bin of a tourist hotel, and had been refilled with toxic home-brew. Or again, it might be the black market. Perhaps the fortunate ones who went off through the western gates were going to pick up the contraband. Or if it wasn't that, it was probably to do with religion, or the monarchist party, or astrology, or numerology, or gambling, or the Moonies. Such huddled, fervent meetings rarely concerned themselves with the new democratic structures, environmental pollution, or the problems of land reform. It was always something illegal, or escapist, or at the very best to do with grubby self-advancement. *And* they didn't look at her.

*

Stefan's grandmother refused to watch the trial, and at first the students were awkwardly aware of her presence. She sat a few metres away in the kitchen, underneath a small framed colour print of V.I. Lenin, which no-one had dared suggest she take down. She was a short, spherical woman with a down-turned mouth accentuated by the loss of several teeth, and the home-knitted cap she wore at all times, even indoors, added to her circularity. Nowadays she spoke little, finding that most questions did not require answers. A nod, a shrug, a held-out plate, occasionally a smile: you could get by with that. Especially when dealing with Stefan and his young friends. How they chattered. Listen to them round the television, gabbling away, interrupting one another, unable to pay attention for more than a moment. Squabbling like a nestful of thrushes. Brains of thrushes, too.

The girl treated her with reasonable politeness, but the other two, especially that cheeky one, Atanas, was it . . . Here he came again, poking his beak round the door, fixing his birdy little eyes on a point above her head.

'Hello, Granny, is that your first husband?'

Another remark that didn't need a reply from her.

'Hey, Dimiter, have you seen this snap of Granny's boyfriend?'

A second thrush from the nest appeared and examined the portrait for longer than necessary.

'He doesn't look very cheerful, Granny.'

'And he looks a bit old for you.'

'I should drop him, Granny. He doesn't look any fun at all.'

None of this required answering.

The previous evening she had wrapped a woollen scarf over her woollen hat, taken the picture off the wall and left the apartment without saying where she was going. She had caught a tram to the Square of the Anti-Fascist Struggle, whose name she continued to use whatever insolent bus-drivers called it, and bought three red carnations from a peasant who at first tried to charge her double on the ground that she was going to the rally and was therefore a Communist and the cause of all his life's problems. Her rare sally into speech shamed him into normalising the price, and she had stood in the square with a few hundred other loyalists, while confident men who were clearly not party members patrolled the edges of the gathering. How long would it be before the Party was banned again, forced to go underground? Before the Fascists resurfaced, and young men searched their attics for the faded green shirts of

54

their Iron Guard grandfathers? Ahead she saw an inevitable return to the oppression of the working class, to unemployment and inflation being used as political weapons. But she also saw, beyond that, the moment when men and women would rise and shake themselves, recovering their rightful dignity and starting again the whole glorious cycle of revolution. She would be dead by then, of course, but she did not doubt that it would come to pass.

*

It was not until the weekend that Peter Solinsky had time to examine the dossier given him by the security chief. Anna Petkanova 1937–1972. Curious how the dates were always attached so that he knew them by heart. The name and the dates, on postage stamps, memorial plaques and concert programmes, on her statue outside the Anna Petkanova Palace of Culture. Only child of President Stoyo Petkanov. Beacon of Youth. Minister of Culture. Photographs of Anna Petkanova as a dimpled Young Pioneer in her red bonnet, as a serious-faced chemistry student with eye applied to microscope, as an overweight young cultural ambassadress receiving bouquets at the airport on her return from foreign trips. An example to women throughout the nation. The very spirit of Socialism and Communism, the embodiment of its future. The youthful Minister inspecting plans for the Palace of Culture now named in her memory. The stouter Minister accepting flowers from folk dancers, sitting attentively in the presidential box at symphony concerts. The positively fat Minister, cigarette in advanced prodding position, listening critically at meetings of the Writers' Union. Anna Petkanova, more than a little overweight, unmarried, keen on cigarettes and banquets, dead at thirty-five. Mourned by the nation. Even the nation's finest heart specialists had been unable to do anything despite the most modern techniques. Her ageing father, bare-headed in the felty snow, standing to attention outside the crematorium as her ashes were scattered. And the plaque on the wall there repeated: Anna Petkanova 1937–1972.

Really, thought Solinsky, as he leafed through Ganin's report, this is trivial stuff. It did not surprise him that the Department of Internal Security had had a file on the President's daughter, that a certain well-placed assistant in the Ministry of Culture reported on a monthly basis, or that the Minister's relationship with that gymnast who had won a silver medal in the Balkan Games should have been closely watched. The gymnast, he seemed to remember, had got offensively drunk at a banquet some weeks after Anna Petkanova's death, and shortly afterwards had been permitted to emigrate, the standard phrase for being woken at dawn and driven to the airport without a change of clothes.

Stoyo Petkanov had declared a week of national mourning for his daughter. They had been very close. After her appointment as Minister of Culture she was increasingly seen at his side, replacing her invalid mother, who apparently preferred to stay in one of the country residences. It was rumoured that Petkanov had been grooming his daughter to succeed him in office. It was further rumoured that the President's daughter had grown so stout because on one of her foreign trips she had become addicted to American hamburgers, and after unsuccessfully trying to instruct the presidential cooks in their manufacture, had taken to having them flown in. Frozen hamburgers in bulk, courtesy of the diplomatic bag.

These rumours were all more or less confirmed by Lieutenant-General Ganin's file, along with the detail that the President's wife had, in her declining years, paid secret visits to the little wooden church in her native village, and that her invalidism was largely caused by vodka. But all this had become history. Anna Petkanova 1937–1972 was dead. So was her mother. Stoyo Petkanov was currently answering the nation on various charges, but having a drunken priest-kissing wife was not one of them. And the gymnast? As far as Solinsky could remember, he had lived in Paris for a while, where his career had not prospered, then had taken a coaching job in a mid-western American city. They said that one night, drunk again, he had stepped out in front of a truck and been killed. Or had that been someone else?

It was all a long time ago. The Prosecutor General pushed aside the file and looked up from his desk. The sun was beginning to set, and its rays were catching the bayonet on the Statue of Eternal Gratitude to the Liberating Red Army. Yes, of course, it was there that he had first set eyes on Anna Petkanova. One May Day the serious-minded chemistry student with eye pressed inspiringly to micro-scope had accompanied her father to the wreath-laying. He recalled a stocky figure, a serious, rather pug face, and hair coiled rope-like on top of her head. At the time, of course, she had seemed unimaginably glamorous, and he would have died for her.

*

In one respect, the trial was like most other trials that had taken place here over the previous forty years: the President of the Court, the Prosecutor General, the defence

57

counsel and the accused – most of all the accused – knew that anything other than a verdict of guilty was unacceptable to higher authority. However, apart from this concluding certainty there were no fixed points, and no legal tradition to follow. In the old days of the monarchy a cabinet minister had occasionally been impeached, and a couple of prime ministers dismissed from office by the roughly democratic method of assassination, but there was no precedent for such a public, open-ended trial of a deposed leader. And although the actual charges were tightly drawn to minimise the possibility of the defendant evading conviction, the President of the Court and his two assessors felt an implied permission, bordering on a national duty, to let the proceedings sprawl. Rules of evidence and questions of admissibility were broadly interpreted; witnesses could be recalled at any time; counsel were allowed to pursue hypotheses beyond normal legal plausibility. The atmosphere was more that of a market than of a church.

Stoyo Petkanov, the old horse-trader, did not mind. In any case, he was rarely interested in procedural minutiae. He preferred the broad defence and the even broader counter-accusation. The Prosecutor General had similar powers to range widely in his cross-examinations and general speculation; all the bench had to do was ensure that this representative of the new government was not too obviously humiliated by the former President.

'And did you, on the 25th of June 1976, grant, or instruct to be granted, or permit to be granted, to the said Milan Todorov, a three-room apartment in the Gold section of the Sunrise complex?'

Petkanov did not answer at once. Instead, he let an expression of amused exasperation seep into his face. 'How do I know? Do you remember what you were doing fifteen years ago between two sips of coffee? You tell me.'

'I am telling you then. I am telling you that you made or permitted to be made such an order in direct contravention of the rules governing behaviour of state officials in respect of housing.'

Petkanov grunted, a sound which normally preluded an attack. 'Do you have a nice apartment?' he suddenly asked the Prosecutor General. When Solinsky paused for thought, he was hustled. 'Come on, you must know, do you have a nice apartment?'

[*I have a shitty apartment. Correction. I have twenty per cent of a shitty apartment.*]

Solinsky had hesitated because he didn't particularly think he did have a nice apartment. He certainly knew that Maria was dissatisfied with it. On the other hand, it came hard, the idea of openly denigrating where you lived. So finally he said, 'Yes, I have a nice apartment.'

'Good. Congratulations. And do you have a nice apartment?' he asked the court stenographer, who looked up in alarm. 'And you, Mr President of the Court, I expect a nice apartment comes with the job? And you? And you?' He asked the deputy judges, he asked State Defence Advocates Milanova and Zlatarova, he asked the chief militia officer, and he didn't wait for an answer. He pointed around the courtroom, there, there, there. 'And you? And you? And you?'

'That's enough,' the President of the Court finally ordered. 'This is not the Politburo. We are not here to be harangued like dummies.'

'Then do not behave like dummies. What are these piddling charges? Who cares whether fifteen years ago some struggling actor was permitted to live in two rooms rather than one? If this is all you can find to accuse me of, then I cannot have done much wrong in thirty-three years as helmsman of the nation.'

[*He said "helmsman" again. I think I'm going to choke.' Instead, Atanas spat cigarette smoke over Stoyo Petkanov.*]

'You would rather be charged', Solinsky felt free to suggest, 'with the rape and pillage of this nation, with economic vandalism?'

'I have no bank account in Switzerland.'

[*It must be somewhere else then.*']

'Answer the question.'

'I have never taken anything out of this country. You talk about rape and pillage. Under Socialism we benefited from a rich supply of raw goods from our Soviet comrades. Now you invite the Americans and the Germans here to rape and pillage.'

'They invest.'

'Ha. They put a small amount of money into our country in order to take a larger amount out. That is the way of capitalism and imperialism and those who allow it are not only traitors but economic cretins.'

'Thank you for your lecture. But you have not told us yet what you would prefer to be charged with. What crimes are you prepared to admit to?'

'How easy it is for you to talk of crimes. I admit I made mistakes. Like millions of my fellow-countrymen, I worked and I erred. We worked and we erred, and the nation advanced. Isolated facts cannot be taken to charge the head of state out of the context of the age, the time. So I am here defending not just myself but also those millions of patriots who worked selflessly for all those years.'

'Then perhaps you would tell the court about these "errors" which you deign to admit, but which are, it seems, conveniently less than crimes?'

'Yes,' said Petkanov, startling the prosecutor. He had thought the defendant incapable of such a simple word. 'I take responsibility for the pre-October 12th crisis, and I am willing for my share of that responsibility to be clarified. I think, perhaps,' he went on, in his most statesmanlike tone, 'I think perhaps I should be tried for the nation's foreign debt.'

'Ah, you are at least responsible for something. You actually remember something and you are also responsible for it. And what do you think might be the appropriate sentence for someone who runs up the nation's foreign debt in a final attempt to hold on to power, so that it now represents two years' salary for every man, woman and child in the country?'

'Much of that is your doing,' replied Petkanov easily, 'since the rate of inflation is I understand currently running at forty-five per cent, whereas under Socialism inflation did not exist, since we used scientific methods to combat it. Naturally at the time of the pre-October 12th crisis, I consulted the leading economic experts of the Party and the State, on whose written reports I relied, but I am willing for my share of the responsibility to be clarified. And then, of course,' he went on with more evident complacency, 'it would be a matter for the judgement of the people.'

'Mr Prosecutor General,' said the President of the Court, 'I think it is time we returned to more immediate business.'

'Very well. Now, Mr Petkanov, did you or did you not, on the 25th of June 1976, grant, or instruct to be granted, or permit to be granted, to the said Milan Todorov, a three-room apartment in the Gold section of the Sunrise complex?'

Petkanov sat down and flapped a dismissive hand. 'Do you have a nice apartment?' he asked of no-one in particular. 'Do you? And you? And you?' He turned on his hard chair and addressed the motherly wardress standing behind him. 'And you?'

[*'I have a rotten apartment,' said Dimiter. 'I have twenty per cent of a really shitty apartment.'*

*'What do you expect? You owe two years' salary to President Bush. Lucky not to be living with the gypsies.'*

*'We worked and we erred. We worked and we erred.'*

*'We certainly erred.'*]

\*

Maria Solinska waited an hour outside the Friendship 1 block before she could get on a bus. No, I do not have a nice apartment, she thought. I want an apartment with more room for Angelina, where the electricity does not go off every two hours, where the water supply does not simply dry up as it did this morning. The whole city seemed to be breaking down. Most of the cars were off the road because of the petrol shortage. Even cars converted to gas were now under plastic shrouds since gas had been restricted to domestic use. The buses ran when a tanker brought oil, when the mechanics could push-start them, when the bandits who drove them deigned to turn up as a change from ducking for black-market dollars.

She was forty-five years old. Still attractive, she thought, although she could make no sure deduction from Peter's intermittent zeal. During the Changes people had been too busy, or too tired, to make love: that was another thing which had broken down. And afterwards, when they did, they were scared of the consequences. During the last statistical year, the number of live births had been exceeded both by the number of abortions and by the number of deaths. What did that tell you about a country?

Really, the Prosecutor General's wife should not be expected to take a bus to the office and be hemmed in by fat peasant rumps. She had always worked hard and done her best, it seemed to her. Papa had been a hero of the Anti-Fascist Struggle. Her grandfather had been one of the earliest party members, had joined before Petkanov himself. She had never met him, and for years he had scarcely been referred to, but since the letter arrived from Moscow they could be proud of him again. When she showed the certificate to Peter he had refused to share her pleasure, grumpily commenting that two wrongs did not make a right. That was typical of his recent behaviour, which was quietly, smugly triumphant.

She had married him at twenty. Almost at once his father had done something stupid; people said he had been lucky to escape with exile to the country. And then, at almost the same age, Peter had left the Party, stupidly, provocatively, without even asking her advice. There was something unstable about him, something that sought trouble, just as his father had sought it. And then he'd applied to prosecute Stoyo Petkanov! A middle-aged professor wanting to play the hero! Pathetic. If he lost, he would be humiliated; even if he won, half the people would still hate him, and the other half would say he should have done more.

*

Lieutenant-General Ganin arrived, as before, with a manila folder stuck out in front of him. Perhaps he woke up like that, and the only way to get rid of his condition was to come and see the Prosecutor General.

'We trust, sir, that the course of the trial is proceeding according to your best expectations.'

'Thank you. Tell me about it.' Solinsky reached out and simply took the folder, jerking the security chief into commentary.

'Yes. Report of our investigation into work done at the Special Technical Branch in Reskov Street. Mainly in the period 1963 to 1980, at which point the branch was transferred to the north-east sector. Many of the reports from Reskov Street have remained intact.'

'Pride in their work?'

'Who can tell, Mr Prosecutor?' The General stood stiffly and anxiously before him, more like a provincial lieutenant than a key figure in the restructuring of the country.

'General, on another matter . . . '

'Yes, sir?'

'Do you happen to know . . . It isn't relevant, I just wondered if you knew what became of that student, the one with the beard, who kissed you in the snow.'

'Kovachev. As a matter of fact I do. He organises the visa queue for the US Consulate.'

'You mean, he works for the Americans?'

'No, no. Haven't you seen them, the men in the Square of St Vassily the Martyr? They're queuing for the US Consulate.'

'I don't understand.'

'They don't want to stand in the street, outside the building. They're ashamed, or afraid people will disapprove, or they'll get into trouble. Something like that. So they organise their own queue in the public gardens, by the western gates. Kovachev runs it. You're given a number, and every morning you turn up to see if you've reached the head of the queue. If you haven't, you come back the next day. No-one cheats. Everyone obeys him. He's quite an organiser.'

'We need him on our side.'

'He won't come. I've tried. He sent me a postcard when I got these.' Ganin automatically touched his shoulder, as if his wife had sewn two golden pips on his civilian suit. 'It said: GIVE US GENERALS, NOT BREAD.'

Peter Solinsky smiled. This Kovachev sounded quite a character. Unlike his stodgy general. 'So where were we?'

Ganin resumed his stiffness. 'It seemed that you would be interested in our summary of the research conducted in Reskov Street as it pertained to the effects achieved in the area of the inducement of simulated illness.'

'Specifically?'

'Specifically, inducement of the symptoms of cardiac arrest by oral or intravenous drug.'

'Anything more?'

'Anything more?'

'Any evidence of specific use in individual cases of this research work?'

'No, sir. Not in this file.'

'Well, thank you, General.'

'Thank you, Mr Prosecutor, sir.'

*

They had spent another long afternoon getting nowhere. It was like squeezing a sponge: mostly the sponge was dry, but on the rare occasions when it wasn't, the water ran straight through your fingers. Perfectly well-attested examples of the former President's colossal greed, his brazen acquisitiveness, his kleptomania and furious embezzling, just seemed to vanish in open court before the eyes of several million witnesses. That farm in the north-west province? A birthday present from the grateful nation on the twentieth anniversary of his appointment as Head of State, but in any case a gift only for his lifetime, and he rarely went there, and if he did it was only in order to entertain foreign dignitaries and thus advance the cause of Socialism and Communism. That house on the Black Sea? Offered him by the Writers' Union and the Lenin Publishing House in acknowledgement of his services to literature and in return for his waiving of half the royalties on his *Collected Speeches, Writings and Documents* (32 volumes, 1982). That hunting lodge in the western hills? The Communist Party, in recognition of the fortieth anniversary of the President's successful application for a party card, had generously voted . . . and so on, and so on.

As the case proceeded, Petkanov seemed to get more unpredictable, not less. The Prosecutor General never knew, at the start of a session, if the defendant was going to respond to him with flagrant aggression, joviality, banal philosophy, sentimentality or stubborn muteness, let alone when or why he might switch from one mode to another. Was it some bizarre strategic ploy, or a true indication of a deeply vacillating personality? In his car on the way to the Ministry of Justice, bearing a folder of superficially incriminating affidavits, Peter Solinsky reflected that his plan of getting to know Petkanov, the better to predict his moves, had so far made little progress. Would he ever come to grasp the man's character?

When he reached the sixth floor he found the former President, as if choosing his mood deliberately to annoy, at his most buoyant. What, after all, was Stoyo Petkanov but a normal person with a normal character who had lived a normal life? And why should this not make him the very spirit of cheerfulness?

'Peter, you know, I was just remembering. When I was a boy, I used to go on outings with the Union of Communist Youth. I remember the first time we climbed Rykosha Mountain. It was late October, and snow had already fallen, and you could not see the summit of the mountain from the city because of the cloud level.'

'You can't see it all the year round now,' Solinsky commented. 'Because of the pollution. Such advances we have made.'

'And we climbed all morning.' Petkanov was unperturbed by the interruption; his story ran on tramlines. 'The ground underfoot was rough, with many boulders, and the track was not always clear, and several times we had to cross the river of stones. It's some . . . geological thing, I don't know the name for it. Then we entered the cloud, and for some distance we couldn't see where we were going, and we were glad that the path was clearly marked, that others had gone before us.

'We were beginning to get hungry and a little disheartened, though none of the comrades complained, and our boots were wet and our muscles aching, when all of a sudden, we came out of the cloud. And there, above the cloudline, the sun was shining, the sky was blue, the snow was beginning to weep, and the air was pure. Spontaneously, without anyone planning it, we all burst into "Stepping the Red Pathway", and just sang ourselves to the top of the mountain, linking arms and marching together.'

Petkanov looked across at his visitor. For decades the story had provoked sighing nods of assent and wiped-away tears; all Solinsky offered him was black-eyed belligerence.

'Spare me your cheap analogies,' said the Prosecutor General. God, he had listened to them all his life, the parables, the exhortations, the made-to-measure moralities, the scraps of peasant wisdom. He quoted one that came haphazardly to mind. *'To plant a tree, you must first dig a hole.'*

'That is true,' replied Petkanov benignly. 'Have you ever seen a tree planted without a hole being dug?'

'No, I probably haven't. On the other hand I've seen all too many holes dug where they forgot to plant the bloody trees.'

'Peter, son of my old friend. It would be a mistake to imagine that I know nothing. I know that people live by what you call cheap analogies.'

'I'm glad you said that. We always knew that deep down you despised the people, that you never trusted them. That's why you spied on them all the time.'

'Peter, Peter, you may be familiar with my voice, but you really should try to hear what I actually say. It might be useful to you in your mighty role as Prosecutor General, apart from anything else.'

'So?'

'So, what I said was, I know that people live by *what you call* cheap analogies. It is not I who despise them for doing so, but you. Your father was for some time a theoretician. Does he have nice theories about bees nowadays? You yourself are an intellectual, everyone can see that. I am merely a man of the people.'

68

'A man of the people whose collected speeches and documents run to thirty-two volumes.'

'Then, a hard-working man of the people. But I know how to speak to them, and how to listen.' Solinsky did not even begin to protest. He was beginning to feel a certain weariness. Let the old man chatter on, they weren't in court any more. He didn't believe anything Petkanov said, and he doubted if the former President did either. Was there a rhetorical term to denote this kind of lop-sided conversation, in which hypocritical monologue met contemptuous silence? 'Which means that I know what the people want. What do people want, Peter, can you tell me that?'

'You seem to have appointed yourself the expert today.'

'Yes, indeed, I am the expert. And what do people want? They want stability and hope. We gave them that. Things might not have been perfect, but with Socialism people could dream that one day they might be. You – you have only given them instability and hopelessness. A crime wave. The black market. Pornography. Prostitution. Foolish women gibbering in front of priests again. The so-called Crown Prince offering himself as saviour of the nation. You are proud of these swift achievements?'

'There was always crime. You just lied about it.'

'They sell pornography on the steps of the Mausoleum of the First Leader. You think that is funny? You think that is clever? You think that is progress?'

'Well, he isn't inside to read it.'

'You think that is progress? Come on, tell me, Peter.'

'I think,' replied Solinsky, who despite his weariness retained his lawyer's instinct for leverage, 'I think it's appropriate.' Petkanov looked at him sharply. 'The First Leader specialised in pornography, I'd say.'

'There is no comparison.'

'Ah, but there is, an exact one. You said you gave the people hope. No, what you gave them was fantasy. Big tits and huge cocks and everyone screwing one another endlessly, that's what your First Leader was selling, its political equivalent anyway. Your Socialism was just such a fantasy. More of one, in fact. At least there's some truth in what they're selling outside the Mausoleum nowadays. Some truth in that muck.'

'Who's going in for cheap analogies now, Peter? And how delightful to hear the Prosecutor General defending pornography. You are no doubt equally proud of the inflation, the black market, the whores on the streets?'

'There are difficulties,' Solinsky admitted. 'This is a period of transition. There have to be painful readjustments. We must understand the realities of economic life. We must make goods that people want to buy. Then we shall achieve prosperity.'

Petkanov cackled delightedly. 'Pornography, my dear Peter. Tits and cocks. Tits and cocks to you too.'

*

'You know what I think?'

'You think we should stop watching, Dimiter.'

'Yes, but now I know why I think that.'

'Beer, please.'

'It's like this. We were brought up, weren't we, in school and with the newspapers and television and our parents, or some of them anyway, to think that Socialism was the answer to everything. I mean, that Socialism was right, was scientific, that all the old systems had been tried and didn't work, and

70

that this one, this one we were lucky enough to live under, this one was . . . correct.'

'No-one thought that, Dimiter, not really.'

'Maybe not, but that's what we thought other people thought, didn't we, until we knew, until we found out that most of them were just pretending. And then we realised, didn't we, that Socialism wasn't an unanswerable political truth, and that there are two sides to every question.'

'We realised that with our mother's milk.'

'Yes, there's always a choice of two.'

'Very funny, Atanas.'

'So what I'm trying to say, watching this trial, day after day, listening to the prosecution, listening to the defence, waiting for the judges to decide, is that it's being . . . it's being far too nice to him.'

'Because the charges are so trivial.'

'No, not that at all. Because the whole thing doesn't represent reality. Because there comes a point when there aren't two sides to every question any more, there's only one side. All that's coming out of his mouth is lies and hypocrisy and irrelevant shit. It shouldn't even be listened to.'

'We should have had a moral trial?'

'No, nothing at all. We should just have said, this is a question which doesn't have another side. Just *holding* a trial is giving him false credit, is admitting that even in this case, even in this worst of cases, there is another side to the story. There isn't. End. With some questions, there's one side only. End.'

'Bravo, Dimiter. Give him a beer.'

They were silent for a while. Then Vera said, 'We're at Stefan's tomorrow. Normal time.'

*

'Lieutenant-General, anyone would think you were working for a verdict of not guilty against the former President.'

'Mr Prosecutor?' The Head of the Patriotic Security Forces was bemused.

'Well, you always arrive when I am preparing my cross-examinations.'

'I shall call later.'

'No, no. Just tell me.'

'Notes concerning Central Policy for the years 1970 to 1975.'

'I didn't know there'd been one.'

'There was much dissatisfaction expressed during that period ... No, that's to say, there was much dissatisfaction expressed during the first half of that period with the performance and ambitions of the Minister of Culture.'

Solinsky allowed himself a smile. Really, this soldier had turned himself too successfully into a bureaucrat. 'The security forces disapproved of certain Prokofiev symphonies?'

'No. Well, not exactly, though now you mention it there was much criticism of the programme for the Second International Jazz Congress.'

'I thought the Party approved of jazz as the true voice of an oppressed people suffering under international capitalism?'

'They did. That is repeated more than once. But the particular individualism of one oppressed performer, coupled with a personal interest in his welfare by the Minister of Culture, was held to be detrimental to the future of Socialism.'

'I see.' Perhaps there was a vestigial sense of humour lurking beneath this rounded suit. 'But anyway?'

'But anyway. The personal ambitions of the Minister of Culture were considered dangerous and anti-socialist. Her taste for imported personal goods was held to be decadent and anti-socialist.'

'And imported personal musicians?'

'That too. And the President's own ambitions and wishes concerning his daughter, according to these preliminary notes towards a final report which has not yet come to light, were also deemed detrimental to the interests of the State.'

'Were they?' Now that was interesting. It had little to do with Criminal Law Case Number 1, but it was distinctly interesting. 'Are you saying that the Department of Internal Security murdered her?'

'No.'

'What a pity.'

'I do not have the evidence to say that.'

'But if you found such evidence?'

'I would give it to you, naturally.'

'General, how far would you say the DIS was controlled in those days?'

Ganin reflected for a while. 'I would say about as much as it always is. Always was, I mean. In some areas there was strict control and reporting. In others, general operational approval but no detailed reporting. And in special areas the DIS acted according to their own understanding of what they perceived to be the best security interests of the State.'

'You mean, they knocked people off?'

'Certainly. Not many, as far as we can tell. And not for some years, anyway.'

'No doubt a shortage of fingerprints.'

'Exactly.'

Solinsky gave a slow nod. Reports shredded. Fingerprints wiped. Bodies long gone to the crematorium. Everyone knew what had happened, everyone had known at the time. Yet when people like him were trying to make a succession of charges stick against the man who ran the whole business, it was as if nothing of the sort had occurred. Or as if what had occurred was in some way normal, and hence almost forgivable. The conspiracy of normality, even in crazy times.

And because everyone knew what had happened, everyone had in some unspoken way approved of it. Or was that too sophisticated? Ascribing guilt to everybody was another popular modern conspiracy. No, people had not spoken largely because of fear. Thoroughly justifiable fear. And one part of his job, every day now, on television, was to help expunge that fear, to reassure people that they would never have to give in to it again.

*

Stoyo Petkanov was chuckling as he climbed into the Zil on the steps of the People's Court. Hadn't been in one of these for years. He'd always used a Mercedes himself, in his last years anyway. That Chaika they'd given him up to now was all right, if a little heavy in the suspension. Then this morning, on some excuse, they'd sent this shitty Zil limo from the Sixties. Well, it would take more than that. They could have sent a jeep and he'd still have been in a good humour. What counted was what happened in court. And he'd had another good day. That skinny, pop-eyed intellectual they'd put up against him was losing hair by the hour.

74

The old fox was leading them a merry dance.

He settled back in the unfamiliar bench seat and began to share this reflection with his escort.

'The thing about an old fox', he began, 'is that . . . '

A tram on the boulevard outside came to a halt in a squeal of soprano steel. The convoy stopped. Ha, everything breaks down under them. Can't even run the buses. He scrutinised the crowd behind a zig-zag of ineptly arranged crush barriers. They're letting them get closer than they used to, he thought; closer at least than when he had the Mercedes.

Petkanov noticed some young hooligans behind the nearest barrier shaking their fists at him. I put those shoes on your feet, he answered them silently, I built the hospital in which you were born, I built your school, I gave your father a pension, I kept the country free of invasion, and look at you, fucking scum, daring to wave your paws at me like that. But now they were doing more than that. Two of the barriers had sprung apart and some thugs were running towards the car. Shit. Shit. The fuckers. The double-crossing weasels. That's why they'd given him the Zil, that's how they'd decided to do it, right out in the open . . . then his face smacked the worn red carpet in the well of the car and a militiaman's weight kept him fastened there. He heard a thunderous metallic pounding, and suddenly the carpet burnt his face as the Zil wrenched itself into speed and swerved screechingly round the stalled tramcar. He was kept pinned to the floor until they were back in the sunken courtyard at the Ministry of Justice (formerly Office of State Security).

'Oh God,' said the soldier as he climbed off him, 'Grandfather's shat himself.' He laughed. The driver and the other militiaman joined in.

'The shit's in the other trouser leg now,' commented the driver.

Then they humiliated him all the way back to the sixth floor, leading him the long way round, displaying him to everyone they met, and trying to think up a new phrase every time. 'Uncle's done a nuisance in his knickers.' 'Potty time for the President.' Each different expression, however feeble, made them laugh even more. Finally, they took him to his room and let him clean himself up.

Half an hour later Solinsky arrived. 'I apologise for the momentary lapse in security.'

'They bungled it. You should have been displaying my body to the American media by now.' He imagined the lying headlines. He remembered the Ceausescus, their splayed bodies. Tracked down and hurriedly shot after a secret trial. Nail down the vampires, quick, quick. Nicolae's body, the very body he'd hugged on many a state occasion, emptied of life. The collar and tie still neat, and an ironic, half-smiling expression on those lips that he, Stoyo Petkanov, had many times kissed at the airport. The eyes were open, he remembered that detail. Ceausescu was dead, his corpse was displayed for Rumanian television, but his eyes were still open. Had no-one dared close them?

'It was not what you thought,' said Solinsky. 'Just a few kids who wanted to bang on the car roof. They didn't have a weapon between them.'

'Next time. Next time you'll let them.' The old man lapsed into silence. Solinsky had heard about the former President shitting himself. For almost the first time he looked shrunken and humbled, just an old man sitting at a deal table with a half-finished pot of yoghurt in front of him.

'They loved me,' he said unexpectedly. 'My people loved me.'

Solinsky wondered whether to let that go. But why should he? Just because a tyrant had messed his trousers. He was the Prosecutor General at all times, he should remember that. So he answered, slowly and emphatically, 'They loathed you. They feared you and they loathed you.'

'That would be too easy,' Petkanov countered. 'That would be too convenient for you. That is your lie.'

'They loathed you.'

'They told me they loved me. Many times.'

'If you beat someone with a stick and order them to say they love you, and keep on beating them and beating them, sooner or later they will tell you what you want to hear.'

'It was not like that. They loved me,' Petkanov repeated. 'They called me Father of the People. I dedicated my life to them and they recognised it.'

'*You* called yourself Father of the People. The security police held up banners, that was all. Everyone hated you.'

Ignoring Solinsky, the former President stood up, walked to his bed and lay down. He said to himself, to the ceiling, to Solinsky, to the deaf-mute militiaman, 'They loved me. That is what you cannot bear. That is what you will never come to terms with. Remember it.' Then he shut his eyes.

In repose he seemed to regain his toughness and stubbornness; the flesh relaxed in folds, but the bones got harder, more prominent. As Peter Solinsky was about to look away, he spotted a terracotta dish beneath the low bed, with a plant straggling out across the floor. So the rumour was true. Stoyo Petkanov really did sleep with a wild geranium under his bed, superstitiously imagining that it brought good health and a long life. It was just a dictator's silly whim, but at that moment it terrified the prosecutor. Good health and a long life. Petkanov liked to boast that both his father and grandfather had lived to be centenarians. What would they do with him for the next twenty-five years? Peter had a sudden, nauseating vision of the President's future rehabilitation. He saw a television series, *Stoyo Petkanov: My Life and Times*, starring a genial nonagenarian. He saw himself cast as a villain.

The former President began to snore. Even in this he was not predictable. His snore had no frailty to it, or even comedy; instead it was dismissive, almost imperious. Obediently, the Prosecutor General left.

\*

He had been disappointed with the others. Scuttling away, dying, getting ill. Like a good peasant, he despised illness. They had gone soft, got old. What were those lines he had learnt in Varkova? That had been a test of endurance. Hard labour, beatings from the warders, and the constant fear of a visit from the Fascists with their green shirts and whirling weapons. A commando of the Iron Guard had left six comrades dead in their cells while the prison officers played cards. He who has learned in the tough school of Varkova, Petkanov was fond of saying, will never give up the cause of Socialism and Communism. And what had been whispered to him in his first week there, by a comrade in the exercise yard?

> What the echo of the wall tells
> Is the rotting of the stone and not the souls

78

He had kept the faith. His country had been a model of Socialism, the most loyal ally of the Soviet Union until the betrayals and the weaknesses began. How strong they had been only a short while ago, how united. What respect the world had offered them, what fear. The firm and decisive fraternal action of 1968 had shown the world. Fascist America was being humiliated in its imperialist adventuring in Vietnam, Socialism was gaining ground everywhere, in Africa, in Asia, in Europe. It was a time of great hope, when the leaders stood proudly shoulder to shoulder.

Now look at them. Erich running away to Moscow, holing up like a rat in the Chilean Embassy, waiting for a plane to North Korea. Kadar dead after the betrayal of opening his frontier: you could never trust a Hungarian. Husak dead too, eaten up by a cancer, gibberingly accepting the last rites from a priest in a frock, beaten down by that scribbler he should have banged up for life. Jaruzelski not up to it, joining the other side, saying he now believed in capitalism. Ceausescu, at least he went down fighting, if running away and being executed by firing squad counts as fighting. He was always a mad hog, Nicolae, out for the main chance, playing both sides against the middle, refusing to join the fraternal action of 1968; but at least he had a bit of spine and tried to hold things together until the end.

And then, worst of all, there was that weak fool in the Kremlin who looked as if a bird had shat on his head. Getting into that publicity duel with Reagan. Please let me give away some more SS-20s – now will you put me on the cover of *Time* magazine? Man of the Year. Woman of the Year, thought Petkanov. The Russians weren't even up to running a vodka stall nowadays. Look at that attempted coup of theirs. Pathetic of Gorbachev to get caught by it. Pathetic of the loyalists not to do the obvious things – take out the radio and television, take out the newspapers, take out the parliament buildings, neutralise the dangerous figures. And what did they do? They let that fascist Yeltsin make a hero of himself. What had happened to all the lessons of history when not even the Russians could organise a coup?

And that left him. He had seen it coming, seen the possibility at least, ever since Comecon hiked the oil price in 1983. Then Gorbachev started prancing round the West looking for dollars and goodwill. And now everything was fucked. Gorbachev was fucked – off to be a professor in the United States, they said, getting his tip, thank you Mr President sir. The Soviet Union was fucked into little pieces, the DDR was fucked, Czechoslovakia would snap like a carrot, Yugoslavia was fucked from stem to stern. Look what had happened to the DDR. The capitalists marched in, bankrupted everything, declared it inefficient, threw everyone out of work, picked up all the nice old houses for themselves as second homes, brought every single law into line with capitalist law, and that was it, the DDR fucked. That blonde bitch runner who won those athletics championships, she was all that was left of the DDR. Easterners: fourth-class citizens, despised, unemployed, laughed at for their little cars. Zoo exhibits.

And that left him. 'What the echo of the wall tells/Is the rotting of the stone and not the souls.' He had been in prison before, that was where it had all started, and his soul had not rotted then. Nor had it rotted now. He was never going to crawl away to a priest and die like Husak or scuttle off to the Kremlin like Erich. The new government of plant-loving Fascists had wanted to put him on trial. They knew just what they needed: a weak old man confessing his crimes, pleading guilty to anything in exchange for his life. And he had played it just right in the preliminary interrogations. Refused to co-operate, said he didn't acknowledge their authority, denounced their bourgeois justice, all the time wearily repeating that his only wish was to be allowed to retire to the country and live out his last years in peace. He did this day after day, until they were absolutely sure of one thing, which was that they ached to put him in court. His plan all along.

He didn't care what happened to his life, but he did care what happened to his faith. They were selling pornography outside the Mausoleum of the First Leader. The priests were dancing on the tables. Foreign capitalists were sniffing round the country like dogs on heat. The Crown Prince, as the newspapers had started calling him again, was eyeing his family's palaces and saying of course he wouldn't come back as monarch, just as a businessman trying to help his country if that was permitted. And then he sent his wife on ahead and when she went to a football match no-one watched the game. All this talk about people wanting a referendum on the return of the monarchy, as if it hadn't been decided years ago. The usual tricks. Why didn't the newspapers publish that photograph of the Crown Prince's three uncles in the uniform of the Iron Guard?

And that left him, Stoyo Petkanov, Second Leader, helmsman of the nation, defender of Socialism. That cunt Gorbachev had fucked it, fucked everything. Came here on his royal visit, waving his two little words in the air and expecting everyone to applaud. Telling us at the same time that unfortunately he would no longer be able to accept our money in exchange for his oil. Hard currency only. The irony of the Chairman of the Central Committee of the

Communist Party of the Union of Soviet Socialist Republics soliciting American dollars from the leader of his staunchest socialist ally appeared to be lost on him. When told that the nation had very few dollars, Gorbachev replied that the way to discover dollars was to restructure the country with more openness.

He had been proud of what happened next. 'Comrade Chairman,' he had said, 'I have a proposition, a restructuring of my own to suggest. My country is currently undergoing certain temporary difficulties, the reasons for which we both acknowledge. Our two nations have always striven most closely together in following the socialist path. We were your loyal ally in opposing counter-revolutionary forces in 1968. Yet you come here and announce that our currency will no longer be valid with you, that a new separation is to be put between our two countries. This does not strike me as necessary or, if I may say so, fraternal. I have a different idea to put to you, a different vision of the future. I propose, instead of our two nations each stepping out on its own red pathway as we cross this river of stones we have just encountered on the great mountain, I propose, instead of this, that we draw closer.'

He could see Gorbachev's interest was fully roused. 'What do you mean?' the Russian asked.

'I propose a full political integration between our two states.'

Gorbachev was not expecting this. It had not been in the preliminary protocols. He did not know how to handle the situation. He had come to tell the Second Leader what to do in his own country, and decided beforehand that he was dealing with some idiot comrade of the old school, one who did not understand the way the world was moving. But *he*,

Stoyo Petkanov, he had been the one with the plan, and the Russian had not liked that.

'Explain yourself,' Gorbachev had said.

He had explained himself. He had talked of the nation's continued and loyal striving towards Socialism, internationalism and peace. He referred to his people's historic struggle and their continued aspirations. He candidly addressed the contradictions which can emerge and which can harm the interests of social construction if they are not investigated and if purposeful action is not taken by the Party and the State for their settlement. Parenthetically, but yet centrally, he recalled his adolescent epiphany on Mount Rykosha. In conclusion, he spoke rousingly of the future, of its challenges and opportunities.

'As I understand it,' his visitor had finally said, 'you are proposing that your country be incorporated into the USSR as the sixteenth republic of that Union.'

'Exactly.'

*

The defence was offered a day's adjournment after the regrettable incident at the courtroom gates. State Advocates Milanova and Zlatarova, whom the former President had unexpectedly started to consult on minor business, were in favour; but Petkanov overruled them. And the next morning, as the Prosecutor General pressed him yet again about his notorious personal greed, his mood was benign, his innocence ebullient.

'I am an ordinary man. I need little. I have never, during all my years as helmsman, asked much for myself.'

[*The fool asks much, but he is more of a fool who grants it.*]

'I have simple tastes. I do not require many things.'

[*What can you need when you own the whole country?*'

'More than just the country. Us too. Us.*]

'I have no money hoarded away in Switzerland.'

[*It must be somewhere else then.*]

'When they found Thracian gold on my land, I gave it voluntarily to the National Archaeological Museum.'

[*He prefers silver.*]

'I am not like the imperialist presidents of the United States, who present themselves to their fellow-countrymen as simple folk, and then leave office laden down with riches.'

[*Us, us.*]

'I have been awarded many international honours, but I have always accepted them on behalf of the Party and the State. I have often given money to the nation's orphanages. When the Lenin Publishing House insisted that I took royalties on my books, since otherwise writers would not be encouraged to do so themselves, I always gave half away to the orphanages. This was not always publicised.'

[*We are the orphans.*]

'My late wife never dressed in Paris fashions.'

[*She should have done. Bag of suet.*

'Raisa! Raisa!*]

'My own suits, for that matter, are made from cloth woven at a communal production centre close to my own home village.'

Solinsky had had enough. At the start of the morning's session, he might have been prepared to let things go quietly. But his tolerance was decreasing daily, and the onset of tiredness he felt was edged with nausea. 'We are

84

not talking about your suits.' His tone was peremptory and sarcastic. 'We do not wish to hear that you consider yourself a paragon of virtue. We are investigating your corruption. We are investigating the way in which you systematically bled this country to death.'

The President of the Court was beginning to feel tired too. 'Be specific,' he urged. 'This is not the place for mere denunciation. You can leave that to the speakers in the public squares.'

'Yes, sir.'

'But what is corruption?' Petkanov suavely picked up the argument, as if Solinsky's irritated outburst had merely been a prompt. 'And why do we not talk about suits?' He stood with his hands on the padded bar, a compact figure, head set low on the shoulders, and questing nose raised to sniff the courtroom air. He seemed the only person with any energy that day; he was the one driving the tribunal along. 'Is not corruption in the eye of the beholder? Let me give you an example.' He paused, knowing that this offer of actual information, set beside his habitual denials and failures of memory, would compel attention. 'You, for instance, Mr Prosecutor General, I well remember that time we sent you to Italy. The middle-Seventies, was it not? You were, or at least you then proclaimed yourself to be, a loyal member of the Party, a good Communist, a true Socialist. We sent you to Turin, you will recall, as part of a trade delegation. We also gave you some hard currency, which was a privilege, the fruits of the labours of your fellow-countrymen. But we gave you some.'

Solinsky looked at the bench. He didn't know what was coming – or at least, he hoped he didn't know what was coming. Why hadn't the President of the Court intervened?

Wasn't this mere denunciation too? But all three judges were complacently sitting on their hands, showing an immoderate interest in Petkanov's tale.

'How, the court might ask, does a good Communist spend the hard currency provided for him by the sweat of the workers and peasants at home? Does he buy socialist books by our fraternal Italian colleagues, books worthy of study? Does he perhaps give some money to a local orphanage? Would he save as much as possible, bring it home and return it to the Party? No, no, no, none of these things. He spent part of it on a nice Italian suit, so that he could be more elegant than his comrades when he returned home. He spent some of it on whisky. And he spent the rest of it,' Petkanov paused again, an old ham who had long ago understood that old hams' tricks work, 'he spent the rest of it on taking a local woman to an expensive restaurant. I ask you simply, is this corruption?'

He waited, nose in the air, rims of his spectacles glinting in the TV lights, and just before anyone was likely to answer, he went on, 'The woman later went back to the Prosecutor General's hotel room, it goes without saying, where she spent the night.'

['*Wow.*'
'*Up the arse. Up the arse.*'
'*Poor old Solinsky. Right up the arse.*']

The prosecutor was on his feet, the President of the Court was consulting with his assessors, but Stoyo Petkanov continued to bellow at his adversary. 'Don't you deny it. I have seen the photographs. She was very well built. I congratulate you. I have seen the photographs. Tell me, what is corruption? I congratulate you. I have seen the photographs.'

The judge brought the session to a hasty close, the TV

director faded down the sound while instructing Camera Number 1 to stay tight on the prosecutor's alarmed features, *the students were momentarily silent*, Stefan's grandmother cackled to herself quietly in the kitchen while the television played to an empty sitting-room, and Peter Solinsky, when he returned home, furious and betrayed, found that a bed had been made up for him on the floor of his study. He would sleep there, with only the distant Alyosha for company, until the end of the trial.

*

And that weak cunt with birdshit on his head had been such a hypocrite, such a betrayer of Socialism. When Gorbachev came on his round of urgent consultations, which consisted of informing his oldest, closest allies that he would drop them down the crapper unless they stumped up some of Uncle Sam's hot, hard dollars, he had offered him the boldest deal in the country's political history.

'Comrade Chairman,' he had said, 'I propose a full integration of our two countries.' What a stroke! At the very time when rumour-mongers and the lackeys of the capitalist press were producing ever more slander about the imminent collapse of Socialism, at that precise moment to be able to say: look, Socialism is growing and developing, look how two great socialist nations join their destinies together, how the Union of Soviet Socialist Republics now has a sixteenth member! How that would have confounded the slanderers!

But Gorbachev had turned his proposal down without even the courtesy of reflection. He had made the same offer to Brezhnev a decade earlier, and at least Leonid had considered it for some months before expressing fraternal regret. Whereas Gorbachev had been contemptuous. 'That is not what we understand by restructuring,' he had replied, going on to suggest that Petkanov's revolutionary plan was motivated by a desire to avoid paying his oil bill.

Now the world could see what that self-important fool meant by restructuring. He meant letting the USSR – what Lenin built, what Stalin and Brezhnev defended – he meant letting all that go fuck itself. He meant letting the republics fuck off whenever it pleased them. He meant bringing the Red Army home from its fraternal stationings. He meant getting on the cover of *Time* magazine. He meant ducking for dollars like a whore in the lobby of the Sheraton Hotel. He meant sucking Reagan's dick and then sucking Bush's. And when the republics thumbed their noses at him, when he let the Soviet Union and the cause of international Socialism be humiliated by those shitty little Baltic states, when he had his very last chance to defend the Union, to save the Party and the Revolution, to send in the fucking tanks for God's sake, how did he react? Like a dimwit *babushka* who sees her potatoes dropping out of a hole in her string bag. Oh, there goes another one, dearie me, well it doesn't matter, there are lots left. Oh, and another one, no, that doesn't matter either, that little tattie wanted to get away anyhow. And oops, another, naughty little spud, still, I wasn't hungry, was I? And the imbecile old *babushka* gets home and the string bag is empty. But it doesn't matter, because *dedushka* hasn't had the strength to raise his hand to her in years. 'All them tatties is gone,' she tells him. 'Let's have warm water again for supper.' 'That's what we had yesterday,' says *dedushka* complainingly. 'You'll get used to it,' she replies, running the tap. 'Anyway, most of them tatties was rotten.'

And that cunt in the Kremlin had been such a hypocrite

too. Of course Petkanov was not suggesting that his proposed political union take place instantly, without discussion, without a full consideration of economic factors. His offer had been, at this stage anyway, primarily an expression of solidarity, goodwill and intent. Whereas Gorbachev had reacted as if his motive was one of short-term economic gain, as if his bold scheme amounted to no more than a desire to get his country's debt cancelled.

And what had been happening all the while? Gorbachev was busy selling the DDR to the Federal Republic. *Selling the East to the West.* Sixteen million socialist citizens put into the biggest slave auction in the history of mankind, with all their land and houses and cattle and enterprises. Why didn't anyone protest about *that*? A few malcontents and hooligans in the last days of Erich's helmsmanship whined about the necessary restrictions on the right to travel. But did anyone complain about being sold like pigs in a farmers' market? Sixteen million citizens of the DDR in exchange for 34 billion Deutschmarks – that was the deal Gorbachev struck with Kohl in one of the vilest and blackest deeds in the history of Socialism. And then, at the end, Gorbachev squeezed an extra 7 billion Deutschmarks out of Kohl, and went home very pleased with himself, idiot *babushka* that he was. Forty-one billion Deutschmarks was the price of betrayal nowadays, Socialism's thirty pieces of silver. And they let him do it. The army, the KGB, the Politburo, between them they put together one feeble botched coup. They let him do it, they let him give it all away.

'What the echo of the wall tells/Is the rotting of the stone and not the souls!' But the smell coming out of Mother Russia recently was the stink of rotting souls.

*

'I think you would like to hear a joke now,' said Atanas.

'How you anticipate our every need.'

'Do I?'

'That's how you'll know to pass me another beer before telling your joke.'

'You have the idleness of a man with two years' national debt around his neck.'

'Get on with it, Atanas.'

'This is a story of the plains, concerning three men whom I shall name Ghele, Voute and Gyore. It is a particularly appropriate tale for those who cannot fetch their own beer. One day, these three worthy peasants were lazing beside the Iskur river and talking generally among themselves, as people are apt to in such stories.

' "Now, Ghele," said one of the others, "if you were a king, and had all the powers of a king, what would you most like to do?"

'Ghele thought for a while and finally said, "Well, that's a tricky one. I think I would make myself some porridge and put into it as much lard as I liked. Then I wouldn't need anything else."

' "What about you, Voute?"

'Voute thought for quite a bit longer than Ghele, and eventually he said, "I know what I would do. I would bury myself in straw and just lie there for as long as I pleased."

' "And what about you, Gyore?" said the other two. "What would you do if you were a king and had all the powers of a king?"

'Well, Gyore thought about this for an even longer time than the others. He scratched his head and shifted around on the bank and chewed on a grassy stalk and thought and thought and got crosser and crosser. In the end, he said,

"Damn it. You two have already picked the best things. There isn't anything left for me." '

'Atanas, is that a joke from the period after the Changes, from the dark days of Communism, or from the earlier age of the fascistic monarchy?'

'It is a joke for all epochs and for all people. *Beer.*'

*

'General?'

'Mr Prosecutor, sir. First, I would like to express . . . '

'Don't. Don't bother, General. Just tell me.'

'The top document, sir. To begin with.'

Solinsky opened the file. The first paper was headed simply MEMORANDUM and dated the 16th of November 1971. There was no indication at the top of any government ministry or security department. Just a half-page typed statement with two signatures attached. Not even signatures, initials. The Prosecutor General read it slowly, discarding the jargon automatically as he went. That was one of the few skills you learnt under Socialism: the ability to filter out bureaucratic distortions of the language.

The memorandum concerned the joint problems of internal dissent and external slander. There were exiles abroad paid by the Americans to broadcast lies about the Party and the government over the radio. And there were weak, easily influenceable people at home who listened to these lies and then attempted to propagate them. Slander of the State, under the criminal law, was a form of sabotage, and to be punished as such. It was at this point that Solinsky's translation broke down. The saboteurs, he read, were to be 'discouraged by all necessary means'.

' "All necessary means"?'

'It is the strongest term,' replied Ganin. 'Much stronger than "necessary means".'

'I see.' Perhaps the General was developing a sense of humour. 'And where does this document come from?'

'From the building formerly occupied by the Department of Internal Security on Lenin Boulevard. But the signatures are worth examining.'

There were two of them. Initials only. KS and SP. Kalin Stanov, then head of the DIS, later found in a stairwell with a broken neck, and Stoyo Petkanov, President of the Republic, Chairman of the Central Committee, titular head of the Patriotic Defence Forces.

'Stanov? Petkanov?'

The General nodded.

'Where did it turn up?'

'As I said, in the building on Lenin Boulevard.'

'A pity Stanov's dead.'

'Yes, sir.'

'Has Petkanov's signature turned up on anything else?'

'Not that we have discovered so far.'

'Any indication that he understood the term "all necessary means"?'

'With respect, Mr Prosecutor . . . '

'Any evidence of specific cases, any specific authorisation, any instruction from the President, any specific reports back to him about what happened to these . . . these presumed saboteurs?'

'Not so far.'

'Then how do you imagine this might help me?' He pushed back his chair and his eyes were shiny olives as he glared sternly at the security chief. 'There are rules of evidence. I am a lawyer. I am a *professor* of law,' he added emphatically. But at that moment he did not feel particularly like one. Years ago a friend of his had seduced a peasant girl, with the help of a few bribes and certain promises he did not intend to keep. The girl, who came from a strict family, finally agreed to go into the woods with him. They had found a quiet spot and started to make love. The girl appeared to thoroughly enjoy the experience, but just as she was approaching her moment of delight, she suddenly opened her eyes and exclaimed, 'My father is a very honest man.' Solinsky's friend said it had taken all his self-control not to burst out laughing.

'Then let me speak to you for a moment as if you were not a professor of law,' said Ganin. He seemed somehow bulkier today, as he sat across the desk from the thin-faced prosecutor. 'We in the Patriotic Security Forces, as I have said, trust that your diligence in Criminal Law Case Number I will be rewarded, despite . . . despite recent embarrassing disclosures. It is important to hold this trial, for the good of the nation. It is equally important that the accused be found guilty.'

'If he is guilty,' Solinsky replied automatically. My father is a very honest man.

'Further, we know that the charges on which he is being tried are not the charges on which he should have been tried but the charges on which he can best be found guilty.'

'This is normal.'

'Further, we know that many other high party officials and assorted criminals have not been brought to trial, so that the former President is, how shall I put it, their representative in court as well.'

'If he were the only one, we could cover him in honey.'

'Exactly. So what you must know – what, sir, you do know – is that the nation expects from this trial something more than a technical verdict of guilty on a charge of minor embezzlement. Which is the direction in which you are heading at the moment, with due respect. The nation expects to be shown that the defendant is the worst criminal in our entire history. This is your task.'

'That is not, alas, a charge under the Criminal Code. But clearly, General, you have some advice for me.'

'It is, I believe, only my job to give you information.'

'Very well, General, then perhaps you could summarise the information you think you are giving me.' Solinsky's tone stayed cool, but he was throbbing. He was on the edge of some braying, voluptuous iniquity. He had shinned up a bronze Stalin and was poised over the moustache with hammer and chisel.

'I would put it this way. During the late 1960s the Department of Internal Security came to believe that the Minister of Culture was a dangerously anti-socialist influence and that her father's intention of designating her officially as his successor was harmful to the best interests of the State. The Special Technical Branch in Reskov Street was working on the inducement of symptoms which counterfeited those of cardiac arrest. On the 16th of November 1971 the President and the head of the DIS, the late General Kalin Stanov, authorised the use of all necessary means against slanderers, saboteurs and anti-state criminals. Three months later Anna Petkanova died of a cardiac arrest from which even our best heart specialists were unable to save her.'

'Thank you, General.' Solinsky was shocked by Ganin's brutal temptation. 'I can tell you that you will not make a lawyer.'

'Thank you, Mr Prosecutor. I can tell you that such is not my ambition.'

Ganin left. My father is a very honest man, repeated Solinsky. My father is a very honest man.

*

On the thirty-fourth day of Criminal Law Case Number 1, before the Supreme Court, evidence was heard from the following, who were summoned by State Advocates Milanova and Zlatarova:

1. State Security Major Ognyana Atanasova, personal nurse to the former President. She testified that the former leader's entire earthly possessions consisted of a single blanket. 'I can tell you in all responsibility that Stoyo Petkanov has never been free with his money,' she said. 'I used to replace his shirt collars, darn his socks and re-tailor his ties as fashion changed.'

2. Former Deputy Prime Minister Pavel Marinov. He testified that at the 1960 Moscow Conference of Communist and Workers' Parties, Chairman Mao told the President that he would make another great helmsman. 'You are very energetic,' said Mao, 'and I shall nominate you for Prime Minister of the International Socialist Republic.'

3. Former Prime Minister Georgi Kalinov. He testified that it was a myth to believe that the former member of the nomenklatura was a predator. He himself at the moment of speaking possessed in local currency the equivalent of twenty American dollars and was trying to make up his mind whether to invest it in the privatisation process or use it to buy a new pair of shoes. He explained that people had thought him well off because he owned three cars, which

95

he had bought at token prices from the Security Protection Department, the body which provided services to top party and state officials. But he did not consider himself an owner since the Security Protection Department had issued explicit directions that the cars were not to be resold. Asked by Defence Advocate Zlatarova whether the same conditions precluding resale would have applied to the eighteen motor cars referred to by the prosecution as having been owned by the defendant, former Prime Minister Kalinov said he was certain that they would have done.

4. Ventsislav Boichev, former member of the Politburo. He testified that the dollars given to his son by the former President were intended to have an educational effect and were to encourage the young man's interest in technology. Asked why his son had spent the money on a Kawasaki and a BMW, Mr Boichev replied that they enhanced the nation's defence capacity since motor-cycling was still a para-military sport. Asked why his son had not bought popular Soviet-made models, Mr Boichev replied that he did not himself own a driving licence and was not competent to speculate further. He wished to add, however, that for his own part he regretted that the Changes had not occurred back in 1968, and said he personally was willing to be crucified on a red star in the name of his country.

5. Velcho Ganev, Finance Minister under Petkanov. He testified that he was entirely confident that the entertainment allowances were entirely lawful. The procedure, however, was 'top secret'. Asked why the lists of those entitled to privileged treatment had been destroyed, Mr Ganev replied that the lists were receipts and not payrolls. It was his understanding of the law that whereas payrolls had

to be preserved for fifty years, the same condition did not apply to receipts.

*

On the thirty-seventh day of the trial, in the public square opposite the People's Court, beneath a bare acacia tree on which fake leaves and blossom had been hung, the Devinsky Society of the capital's second university held a mock auction of memorabilia belonging to the ex-President. Bidders were obliged to declare themselves by name before making their offer, and among those present were Erich Honecker, Saddam Hussein, Emperor Bokassa, George Bush, Mahatma Gandhi, the entire Central Committee of the Albanian Communist Party, Josef Stalin and several claimants of both sexes purporting to be Stoyo Petkanov's secret lover. Bids were only to be made in hard currency. Comrade Petkanov's blanket, described as his 'sole earthly possession' by the auctioneer, was sold to Erich Honecker for 55 million US dollars. Two pairs of darned socks, plus one hair shirt with a new collar personally stapled to it by State Security Major Ognyana Atanasova, went for 27 million US dollars. The pair of pigskin sandals worn by Comrade Petkanov when he had first made contact with the resistance fighters whom he was to command during the Anti-Fascist Struggle were sold for 35 million US dollars to the official representative of the Mythological Museum. A pair of trousers with a large brown stain on the seat, also worn by Comrade Petkanov during the Anti-Fascist Struggle, went unsold. Emperor Bokassa bought the former President's genitalia for one dime, and said he would eat them for dinner. Cheques representing successful bids were placed in the mouth of a large effigy of the Second Leader which presided at the sale. Afterwards the effigy, happily swinging by the neck from a branch of the acacia tree, told journalists that he was well satisfied with the result of the sale and had already given all the money to orphans who wished to take up the para-military sport of motor-cycle riding.

*

On the thirty-ninth day of the trial, Vesselin Dimitrov, who had previously escaped giving evidence because of an unspecified nervous illness, became the last in a group of seven actors to testify. He explained how his father, the deputy regional secretary of a southern province, had approached a member of the President's personal entourage, and asked him to recommend to Comrade Petkanov, who was well known for his patronage of the arts, the case of his son, a loyal Communist and zealous worker with the People's National Theatre, who was also suffering temporary problems in finding accommodation. Two weeks later a three-room apartment in the Sunrise complex had become available, and the actor was able to move in.

'Why did you join the Communist Party in the first place?'

'Because everyone did in my family. It was the way to get on.'

'What did you tell people when you received your apartment?'

'I told them I was lucky. It had suddenly become available. I told them sometimes things worked.'

'The price was substantially reduced. How was this explained?'

'I was told that the apartment came with an artistic subsidy.'

'How did you repay the favour?'

'I don't understand.'

'What did you do in return for obtaining a three-room apartment at one-tenth of its value without even waiting the normal ten, fifteen or twenty years?'

'It wasn't like that. I never paid anybody back.'

'Did you rehearse and appear in the spontaneous mime celebrations which greeted the accused when he stepped outside his palace on his sixty-fifth birthday?'

'Yes, but it was a voluntary decision.'

'Did you appear in private performances for the President and the higher echelons of the nomenklatura?'

'Yes, but it was always a voluntary decision.'

'Did you report back to a contact in the Department of Internal Security on designated individuals in the People's National Theatre?'

'No.'

'Are you quite sure? I warn you the files have survived.'

'No.'

'No you are not sure?'

'No I did not.'

'I can't hear you. Would you project your voice a little more?'

'No I did not.'

'Thank you. Mr President, I request that on the basis of his own testimony Mr Dimitrov be formally charged with corruption, embezzlement and perjury.'

'That request, as I have already explained to you six times, Mr Prosecutor General, is not a matter for this court and is therefore refused.'

[*'Oh, for God's sake.' Atanas spat smoke, this time fogging the face of the Prosecutor General.*

*'Yeah, let's stop.'*

*'It's just actors. They're all actors. It's a fucking comedy.'*

*'Actors, apartments, motorbikes, lunch expenses, shirt collars.'*

*'Stefan?'*

*'No, I want to watch. We've got to.'*

*'We've got to. It's our history.'*

*'But it's BORING.'*

*'History often is when it happens. Then it becomes interesting later.'*

*'You're such a philosopher, Vera. And a tyrant.'*

*'Thank you. Anyway, one day I'll be an old baba in a headscarf and you'll be an old fool dribbling into his beer and our grandchildren will come to us and say, Grandparents, were you alive when they tried the monster? We know you're very, very old, can you tell us about it? And then we'll be able to.'*

*'Tell them about actors and motorbikes, you mean.'*

*'That too. But tell them about him laughing at us. That's what he's always done, that's what he's still doing. Laughing at us. Tell them why it ended up being about actors and motorbikes.'*

*'Tyrant.'*

*'Shh. Watch.'*

*'Who's that? Another actor?'*

*'It's a banker to say that all the money in the presidential account was there by mistake.'*

*'It's a blanket manufacturer to say that they only ever made him one blanket.'*

*'Shut up, boys. Watch.'*]

*

That night Peter Solinsky, who slept badly on his study floor, wandered into the sitting-room and discovered the newly framed certificate of rehabilitation hanging on the wall. Further proof of the distance between himself and Maria.

Her grandfather Roumen Mechkov had been, as they always put it, a loyal Communist and diligent anti-Fascist. In the early 1930s, as the Iron Guard intensified its violent purges, he had accompanied other leading party members into exile in Moscow, where he had remained a loyal Communist and diligent anti-Fascist until some time in 1937, when he had become a Trotskyist deviationist, a Hitlerite infiltrator, a counter-revolutionary agitator, and quite possibly all three simultaneously. No-one had dared ask questions about his disappearance. Roumen Mechkov did not appear in official histories of the local Party, and for fifty years his family had only whispered his name.

When Maria announced her intention of writing to the Supreme Court of the USSR, Peter had opposed the idea. Any discovery she made would only cause her pain. And besides, she could not bring back to life the grandfather she had never known. What he meant, though did not quite express, was that in his view there were only two possibilities. Either Mechkov had betrayed the great cause in which he had believed, or else he had been viciously duped by it. Which would you prefer your grandfather to be, Maria, a criminal renegade or a credulous fool?

Maria ignored her husband's advice, posted her submission, and after almost a year received a reply dated 11th December 1989 from A.T. Ukolov, Member of the Supreme

Court of the USSR. He was able, after investigation, to inform the enquirer that her grandfather, Roumen Alexei Mechkov, had been arrested on 22nd July 1937 and charged with 'being a member of a Trotskyist terrorist organisation and, in this capacity, conspiring to commit acts of terrorism against Comintern leaders and sabotage the USSR'. Interrogated at the Stalingrad (now Volgograd) Regional Department of the People's Commissariat for Internal Affairs, Mechkov had been sentenced to death by firing squad on 17th January 1938, the sentence being carried out the same day. A review of the case, conducted in 1955, had established that there was no evidence against Mechkov apart from the conflicting and unspecific depositions of other persons arraigned in the same case. A.T. Ukolov regretted that there was no indication of a place of burial, and that no photographs or personal papers had been preserved in the records. He was able, however, to confirm that the subject of the submission had been an active and loyal Communist, who on 14th January 1956 had been rehabilitated. A.T. Ukolov enclosed with his letter a certificate to this effect.

And you hang that on the wall, thought Peter. Proof that the movement to which your grandfather dedicated his life slaughtered him as a traitor. Proof that the same movement decided twenty years later that he was not, after all, a traitor but a martyr. Proof that the same movement did not think to inform anyone of this substantial change of status for another thirty-four years. Maria wanted to be reminded of that?

A loyal Communist becomes a Trotskyist terrorist and then a loyal Communist again. Heroes become traitors, traitors become martyrs. Inspirational leaders and helmsmen of the nation become common criminals taken with their hands in the cashbox – until, perhaps, at some dread moment in the future, they become charming nonagenarians on TV chat shows. Peter Solinsky looked at the uncurtained window and saw its blackness fill with opening titles. *Stoyo Petkanov: the Rehabilitation of a Helmsman.* Whether or not such revisionism occurred would partly depend on how he performed in the final week of the trial.

And what did professors of law, prosecuting counsel, husbands, fathers become? What new names would be applied, what unnaming would take place? What chance for any of them in the breaking wave of history?

*

'I will tell you what a man with pretensions to wisdom once said to me.'

The Prosecutor General didn't want to hear. He had come to loathe this man. Before, as a mere citizen, he had hated him objectively, usefully. Hatred of Petkanov had been a constructive, unifying force among oppositionists. But since seeing him close up, since talking and fighting with him, the emotion had changed. His loathing had become personal, furious, snobbish and corroding. Past shame, present detestation, future fear: the mix had begun to consume the prosecutor. He seemed to hate Petkanov now as much as he had ever loved his wife; the leader had taken up all the emotional slack that currently existed in his marriage. And now he waited for some tawdry platitude which the swinish ex-President had picked up from some toiling hero of labour who in any case had probably filched it loyally from the collected speeches, writings and documents of the swinish ex-President.

'He was a musician,' said Petkanov. 'He played in the State Radio Symphony Orchestra. I had gone with my daughter. She took me afterwards to be presented to the players. They had performed well, I thought, so I toasted them. This was in the Revolutionary Concert Hall,' he added, an embellishing detail which for some reason irritated Solinsky like the bite of a horse-fly. Why tell me that, he found himself asking. Who cares in which damn hall you claim to have been impressed by the music? Who cares, what difference does it make? In his rage he heard Petkanov's story continue distantly, through thick curtains. 'And in the few words I spoke I talked of the requirements of art in the political struggle, how artists must join in the great movement against Fascism and imperialism and towards building the socialist future. You can imagine', he said, with a touch of irony well lost on Solinsky, 'roughly what I said. Anyway, afterwards, as I was moving through the orchestra, a young violinist came up to me as I passed. "Comrade Petkanov," he said, "Comrade Petkanov, the people don't care about higher things. They care only for sausage." '

Petkanov looked at the Prosecutor General for his reaction; but Solinsky hardly seemed to be focusing. Eventually, as if coming to, he said, 'I suppose you had him shot.'

'Peter, you are so old-fashioned. So old-fashioned in your criticism. Of course not. We never shot people.' We'll see about that, thought the prosecutor, we'll dig in the grounds of your prison camps, we'll carry out autopsies, we'll get your secret police to squeal on you. 'No. But let's say that his chances of becoming leader of the orchestra were a little diminished after this frank exchange of views.'

'What was his name?'

'Oh, really, you do not expect me . . . Anyway, the

point is this. I did not agree with that rather cynical young man. But I also thought about what he had said. And so, every now and then, afterwards, I would repeat to myself, "Comrade Petkanov, the people need sausage *and* higher things." '

'So?' Such was the wisdom of the Revolutionary Concert Hall. You mutter a few brave words of protest backstage, and if you are not shot then your thought is twisted into some tiny, banal motto by this, by this . . .

'So, I am merely passing on helpful advice. Because, you see, we gave them sausage *and* higher things. You do not believe in higher things, and you do not even give them sausage. There is none in the shops. So what do you give them instead?'

'We give them freedom and truth.' It sounded pompous in his mouth, but it was what he believed, so why not state it?

'Freedom and truth!' replied Petkanov mockingly. 'So those are your higher things! You give women the freedom to come out of their kitchens and march on your parliament and tell you this truth – that there is no fucking sausage in the shops. That's what they tell you. And you call this progress?'

'We will get there.'

'Hmmm. Hmmm. I doubt it. I ask permission to doubt it, Peter. You know, the priest in my village – and he probably was shot, I'm afraid, there were so many criminal elements around at the time, it could easily have happened – the priest in my village used to say, "You don't get to Heaven at the first jump." '

'Exactly.'

'No, Peter, you misunderstand me. Actually, I am not

talking about you. You and your sort have had many jumps already. Many centuries and many jumps. Jump, jump, jump. I am talking about *us*. We have only had one jump so far.'

*

Character. Perhaps that had been his mistake, his . . . yes, his bourgeois-liberal error. The naive hope of 'getting to know' Petkanov. The stubborn yet foolish belief that the exercise of power reflects an individual's character, and that the study of character is therefore necessary and profitable. True at one time, no doubt: true of Napoleon and Caesars and Tsars and Crown Princes. But things had moved on since then.

The assassination of Kirov, that was the key date. Shot in the back with a Nagan revolver in the headquarters of the Leningrad Communist Party on the 1st of December 1934. Stalin's friend and ally, Stalin's comrade. Therefore, as we innocently used to say, therefore the one person in the world who could not possibly have wished or hoped for it, let alone ordered it, was Stalin himself. This was an impossibility in all known political and personal terms. For Stalin to have ordered Kirov's death was not just 'out of character', but beyond our understanding of what character might comprise. Which was precisely the point. We have moved into an era when 'character' is a misleading concept. Character has been replaced by ego, and the exercise of authority as a reflection of character has been replaced by the psychopathic retention of power by all possible means and in mockery of all implausibilities. Stalin had Kirov killed: welcome to the modern world.

Solinsky found he was convinced by this conclusion as long

as he sat calmly in his study looking north, or interrogated the bookcase in his office; but the attempt to see Petkanov as a malign whirr of electrons circling some monstrous vacuum did not survive two minutes in his presence. The old man, shadowed by his wardress, would stand before him arguing, denying, lying, feigning incomprehension; and immediately all the Prosecutor General's primary emotions – curiosity, expectation, bafflement – were back in place. He searched again for character, for old-fashioned, explicable character. It was as if the law itself demanded the cause-and-effect of logical motive and resultant action; the court-room simply declined to admit any tinkering with iron consequentiality.

By mid-afternoon on the forty-second day of Criminal Law Case Number 1, Peter Solinsky decided that the moment had come. Yet another line of enquiry, into the use of official petrol for private purposes, had petered out in squabbles and forgetfulness. 'Very well,' he said, taking a long, opera-singer's breath and picking up another file. During the lunchtime adjournment he had splashed water on his face and combed his hair again. In the mirror he had looked tired. He was tired, from his work, from his marriage, from political anxiety, but mainly from being in the presence of Stoyo Petkanov day after day. How tempting it must have been for those fawning members of the Politburo simply to save energy by agreeing with him.

Now he tried to forget his wife, and Lieutenant-General Ganin, and the TV cameras, and all the promises he had made to himself before the trial began. Enough of being the honourable lawyer who patiently eases truth, like a dandelion leaf, from between the teeth of lies. Perhaps he was tired of doing that too. 'Very well, Mr Petkanov. We have become more than familiar over the many weeks of this criminal case with your defence. Your defence to all charges and accusations. If something illegal was done, then you did not know about it. And if you did know about it, then automatically it was legal.'

Petkanov smiled as his defence advocates rose to object. No, it was rather a good summary by this neurotic pimp of a prosecutor. He waved them to sit down. 'I did nothing that was not approved by the Central Committee of the Communist Party,' he repeated for the hundredth time, 'and ratified in decrees of the Council of Ministers. Everything that I did was entirely legal.'

'Very well. Then let us consider what you did on the 16th of November 1971.'

'How can you . . . '

'I do not expect you to remember, since your memory, as has been amply demonstrated, functions only to recall actions supposedly within the law.' Solinsky held the document given him by Ganin and looked down at it briefly. 'On the 16th of November 1971 you authorised the use of all necessary means against slanderers, saboteurs and anti-state criminals. Would you care to explain what we are to understand by the expression "all necessary means"?'

'I do not know what you are talking about,' Petkanov replied calmly. 'Except that you seem to be approving of sabotage and anti-state crime.'

'On that day you signed a memorandum authorising the elimination of political opponents. That is what "all necessary means" refers to.'

'I do not know what document you are talking about.'

'Here is a copy, and a copy for the court. This is a memorandum from the files of the Department of Internal

Security bearing the signatures of yourself and the late General Kalin Stanov.'

Petkanov barely glanced at the paper. 'I do not call that a signature. I call it a set of initials, quite probably forged.'

'You authorised on that date the use of all necessary means,' Solinsky repeated. 'This authority allowed the departments of both Internal and External Security to take action against political opponents at home and abroad. Opponents like the broadcaster Simeon Popov, who died of a heart attack in Paris on the 21st of January 1972, and the journalist Miroslav Georgiev, who died of a heart attack in Rome on the 15th of March of the same year.'

'Suddenly I am responsible when old men have heart attacks all round the world,' Petkanov replied jovially. 'Did I scare them to death?'

'In the years preceding the executive authority you granted in November 1971, the Special Technical Branch of the DIS in Reskov Street was conducting experiments aimed at producing drugs which, when administered orally or intravenously, produced the symptoms of cardiac arrest. Such drugs were used to disguise the fact that the victim had in fact died as a result of a previous or simultaneous criminal poisoning.'

'Now I am accused of manufacturing drugs? I do not even have an honorary degree in chemistry.'

'During this same period,' Solinsky went on, feeling a noisy exhilaration within him and an intense silence around him, 'the Department of Internal Security, as can be seen from many notes and memoranda, had become increasingly alarmed about the erratic behaviour and personal ambition of the Minister of Culture.'

Solinsky paused, giving himself time, knowing that the

moment had come. He was fuelled by a rich mix of virtue and passion. 'Anna Petkanova,' he added, unnecessarily, and then, as if citing her statue, '1937 to 1972. The DIS frequently reported that her private and public behaviour was of a kind they characterised as anti-socialist. You took no notice of their reports. Further, they were alarmed to discover that you intended to designate the Minister of Culture as your official successor. They discovered this', the Prosecutor General casually threw in, 'by the simple means of bugging your presidential palace. Their dossier on Anna Petkanova records increasing concern about the influence she had, and would continue to have, over you. Anti-socialist influence, as they put it.'

'Absurd,' murmured the former President.

'On the 16th of November 1971 you authorised the elimination of political opponents,' Solinsky repeated. 'On the 23rd of April 1972 the Minister of Culture, who had previously been in excellent health, died quite unexpectedly and at a surprisingly early age of a heart attack. It was pointed out at the time that the nation's leading heart specialists were quickly summoned and did everything they could, but were unable to save her. They were unable to do so for a simple reason: because she was not suffering from a cardiac arrest. Now, Mr Petkanov,' the Prosecutor General continued, his voice hardening to warn off the state defence advocates, who were already on their feet, 'I do not know and frankly do not much care exactly what you knew and exactly what you did not know. But we have it from your own lips that everything you authorised was, under the terms of the New Constitution of 1971 which you introduced, automatically and entirely legal. Therefore, this is no longer a charge I bring merely against you in a personal capacity but against the entire criminal and morally poisoned system at whose head you stood. You killed your daughter, Mr Petkanov, and you are here before us as the representative and chief director of a political system under which it is *entirely legal*, in your much-repeated phrase, *entirely legal* for the head of state to authorise the death even of one of his own ministers, in this case Anna Petkanova, the Minister of Culture. Mr Petkanov, you killed your own daughter, and I ask the court's permission to add the charge of murder to those already listed.'

Peter Solinsky sat down to loudly unjudicial applause, to the drumming of feet, the thumping of desks, and even some raucous whistling. This was his moment, his moment for ever. He had thrust the pitchfork into the earth, one tine on either side of the neck. Look at him snarl and wriggle, spit and fret, pinned out there for all to see, exposed, witnessed, judged. This was *his* moment, his moment for ever.

Daringly, the TV director split the screen. On the left, seated, the Prosecutor General, eyes big with triumph, chin raised, a sober smile on his lips; on the right, standing, the former President in a whirl of fury, banging on the padded bar with his fist, bawling at his defence lawyers, wagging his finger at journalists, glaring up at the President of the Court and his impassive, black-suited assessors.

*

'Worthy of American television,' Maria commented as he closed the apartment door, briefcase in hand.

'You liked it?' He was still breathing extra oxygen after the showdown, the uproar, the honey of applause. He felt he could take on anything. What was his wife's sarcasm when he had defeated the rage of a once-powerful dictator? He could remould anything with words, smooth down his domestic life, sugar Maria's sour disapproval.

'It was vulgar and dishonest, contemptuous of the law, and you behaved like a pimp. I suppose girls came round to your dressing-room afterwards and offered you their telephone numbers?'

Peter Solinsky walked into his small study and gazed out across the smog towards the Statue of Eternal Gratitude. Tonight, no sun caught the gilded bayonet. This was his doing. He had doused the blaze. They could cart Alyosha away now, turn him into teapots and pen-nibs. Or give him to young sculptors and let them rework him into new monuments in praise of the new freedoms.

'Peter.' She stood behind him now and rested her hand on his shoulder. He couldn't tell whether the gesture was meant as apology or consolation. 'Poor Peter,' she added, thereby ruling out apology.

'Why?'

'Because I can't love you any more, and after today I doubt that I can even respect you.' Peter did not respond, did not even turn to see her face. 'Still, others will respect you more and, who knows, perhaps others will love you. I shall keep Angelina, of course.'

'The man was a tyrant, a murderer, a thief, a liar, an embezzler, a moral pervert, the worst criminal in our nation's history. Everyone knows it. My God, even you are beginning to suspect it.'

'If that's the case,' she replied, 'it shouldn't have been difficult to prove without whoring for television and inventing fake evidence.'

'Meaning?'

'Peter, you don't really think the worst criminal in our nation's history would sign such a useful document which Ganin just happened to discover when the prosecution wasn't having the success he'd hoped?'

Naturally, he had considered that, and was ready with his defences. If Petkanov hadn't signed that memorandum, he must have signed something like it. We are only putting into concrete form an order he must have given over the telephone. Or with a handshake, a nod, a pertinent failure to disapprove. The document is true, even if it is a forgery. Even if it isn't true, it is necessary. Each excuse was weaker, yet also more brutal.

In the grim silence of marital despair, he felt sarcasm rise unstoppably to his mouth. 'Well, at least our legal system is a slight improvement on that of the NKVD in Stalingrad around 1937.'

Maria took her hand off his shoulder. 'It's a show trial, Peter. Just the modern version. A show trial, that's all. But I'm sure they'll be very pleased.' Then she left the room, and he continued looking out over the smog, with the growing realisation that she had also left his life.

\*

That imbecile boy prosecutor didn't know what he was up against. If hard labour in Varkova hadn't broken him, when even some of the toughest comrades wet their pants at the thought of a visit from the Iron Guard, he wasn't going to be beaten down by this pitiful cabbage-brained lawyer who was fifth choice for the job. He, Stoyo Petkanov, had sent the boy's father packing without much trouble, kicked him out of the Politburo on a ten-to-one vote and then kept him well watched in his bee-keeping exile. So what chance did this ball-less son of his stand, pottering into court with a silly grin and a bagful of faked evidence?

They – all of them – had this absurd idea that they'd won. Not the trial, which was no more significant than a priest's fart, since they'd arranged the verdict two seconds after deciding the charges; but the historical struggle. How little did they know. 'You don't get to Heaven on the first jump.' Look how many jumps they and their sort had had over the centuries. Jump, jump, jump, like a spotted frog in a slimy pond. But so far *we* have had only one jump, and what a glorious leap it has been. Especially since the whole process began not as Marx had predicted, but in the wrong country and at the wrong time, with all the counter-revolutionary forces lined up to strangle it at birth. Then the Revolution had to be built amid a world economic crisis, defended in a bloody war against Fascism, defended once more against the American bandits with their arms race, and yet . . . and yet we had half the world on our side in a mere fifty years. What a glorious first jump!

Now capitalist filth and newspaper whores were vomiting up their slanders about 'the inevitable collapse of Communism' and 'the inherent contradictions of the system', smirking as they filched the very phrases which had applied for so long – and still applied – to capitalism. He'd read of a bourgeois economist called Fischer who claimed that 'the collapse of Communism signifies the repurification of Capitalism'. We'll see about that, Herr Fischer. What was happening was that just for a brief historical moment the old system was being allowed a last little hop in its slimy frog-pond. But then, inevitably, the spirit of Socialism will shake itself again, and in *our* next jump we shall squelch the capitalists down into the mud until they expire beneath our boots.

We worked and we erred. We worked and we erred. Perhaps, in truth, we had been too ambitious, thinking we could change everything, the structure of society and the nature of the individual, within a couple of generations. He himself had always been less sure about this than some others, and had constantly warned against the resurgence of bourgeois-fascist elements. And he'd been proved right in the last year or two, when all the scum of society had risen to the surface again. But if bourgeois-fascist elements could survive forty years of Socialism, imagine how unquenchably strong in comparison is the soul of Socialism itself.

This movement to which he had dedicated his life could not be snuffed out by a few opportunists, a sackful of dollars and a cunt in the Kremlin. It was as old and as strong as the human spirit itself. It would come back, with fresh vigour, soon, very soon. It might have a different name, a different banner. But men and women would always want to walk that path, that tricky uphill path across the river of stones and through the damp cloud, because they knew that at the end they would burst into the bright sunshine and see the mountain top clear above them. Men and women dreamed of that moment. They would link arms again. They would have a new song – no longer 'Stepping the Red Pathway' as it had been on Rykosha Mountain. But they would sing this new song to the old tune. And they would gather themselves to make that mighty second jump. Then the ground would shake and all the capitalists and imperialists and plant-loving Fascists and filth and scum and renegades and fucking intellectuals and boy prosecutors and Judases with birdshit on their skulls would shit themselves one final, mighty time.

*

'I am Stoyo Petkanov.'

On the forty-fifth day of his trial, the former President addressed the court in his own defence. He stood with one hand on the padded rail, a small, stout figure, his head lifted and jowls tight, checking through his tinted glasses which camera he was on. He coughed, and started again in a firmer, clearer voice.

'I am Stoyo Petkanov. I have received the Collar of the Grand Order "El Libertador" from the Republic of Argentina. The Great Star of the Order of Merit from the Republic of Austria. The Great Collar of the Leopold Order from Belgium. The Great Collar of the Cruizeiro do Sul National Order from Brazil. The Grand Cross of the Order of Valour from the Burundi Republic.'

[*I don't believe this.*]

'And also from the Burundi Republic the Grand Girdle of the National Order.'

[*To keep his stomach in.*]

'The Grand Cross of the Order of Value of Cameroon. The memorial medal to mark the 30th Anniversary of the May Insurrection of the Czechoslovak People. The Great Cross of the Order of Merit of the Centrafrican Republic. The Boyaca Order of Colombia. The Great Cross of Merit from the People's Republic of Congo. The Jose Marti Order from the Republic of Cuba. The Great Girdle of the Makarios Order from Cyprus.'

[*To keep his stomach in.*]

'The Order of the Elephant from Denmark. The title of Doctor Honoris Causa of the Central University of Ecuador. The Order "Great Collar of the Nile" from the Arab Republic of Egypt. The Order of the Great Cross of the White Rose from Finland. The Great Cross of the Legion

of Honour from France. Also the memorial medal Georges
Pompidou. Also the title Doctor Honoris Causa from the
University of Nice.'

['*Who did he fuck in France?*'

'*Everyone. De Gaulle. Giscard. Mitterrand.*']

'The Gold Medal of the Senate and the Memorial Coffer
prepared on the Centennial Anniversary of the French
Senate. The Great Cross of the Equatorial Star Order from
Gabon. The Karl Marx Order from the German Democratic
Republic.'

['*He fucked Honecker.*'

'*He fucked Karl Marx.*'

'*Knock it off, you two.*']

'The Great Cross of the Order of Merit from the Federal
Republic of Germany. The Knight of the Order of the Star
of Ghana. The Great Cross of the Order of the Saviour from
Greece. And the Gold Medal of Athens City. The Great
Cross of the National Order "Truthfulness to the People"
from the Republic of Guinea.'

['*Truthfulness to the People!*'

'*The inhabitants of Guinea are noted for their sense
of irony, Dimiter.*']

'The Pahlavi Order with Collar from Iran. The Order
"The Great Girdle of Merit of the Republic" from Italy.
Also the Aldo Moro Gold Medal. Also the Simba Award for
Peace. Also the Special Gold Medal, first class, Leonardo da
Vinci, of the Rome International Relations Institute. Also
the Gold Plaquette of the Piedmont Regional Junta. The
Great Cross of the National Order of the Ivory Coast. The
Al-Hussein Bin-Ali Collar from Jordan. The Order "The
Republic's Flag", first class, from the Democratic People's
Republic of Korea. The Moubarak the Great Collar from

Kuwait. Also the Silver Plaquette of Kuwait University. The Order of Lebanese Merit. The Great Girdle of the Order of Pioneers from the Republic of Liberia.'

[*'To keep his stomach in.'*]

'The Great Collar of the Mahammaddi Order of Morocco. The Great Girdle of Mauretanian National Merit. The Medal "Champion of World Peace of the 20th Century" from Mauritius. The Great Collar of the Mexican Order of the Aztec Eagle. The Jubilee Gold Medal issued on the Fifth Anniversary of the Independence of Mozambique. The Order of St Olav from Norway. The Medal of Amsterdam City offered by the Mayor. The Nishan-i-Pakistan Order. Also the Pakistan Jubilee Medal Quaid-l-Azam. The Great Cross of the Order of the Sun from Peru. Also the title Doctor Honoris Causa of the National Engineering University of Peru. The Order Sikutana, first class, from The Philippines. The Great Cross of the Santiago Order from Portugal. The Equestrian Order of San Marino. The Great Cross of the National Order of the Lion of Senegal. The Great Girdle of the Omayds from the Syrian Arab Republic.'

[*'I didn't say anything.'*]

'The Knight of the Star of Somalia with Big Girdle.'

[*'Ppffffffkkkkk.'*]

'The Order Civil Merit with Collar from Spain. The Order Collar of Honour from Sudan. The Seraphim Royal Order from Sweden. The Great Girdle of the Order of Independence from Turkey. The Diploma of Citizen of Honour and the Gold Key of Ankara City. The Knight of the Great Cross of the Bath Order from the United Kingdom.'

[*'He fucked the Queen of England.'*

*'Yeah. In the bath.'*

*'He'd do anything for his country.'*]

'The Lenin Order from the USSR.'

[*'Now we're talking. He really fucked Lenin.'*

*'Does your granny know, Stefan?'*

*'And Stalin.'*

*'And Khrushchev.'*

*'And Brezhnev.'*

*'Lots of times. And Andropov.'*

*'And . . . who was that other fucker?'*

*'Chernenko?'*

*'And Chernenko.'*

*'He didn't fuck Gorbachev.'*

*'Gorbachev wouldn't fuck him. Not after he'd been with all the others. Think what he must have picked up.'*

*'He probably gave it to the Queen of England.'*

*'No. That's why she made him do it in the bath.'*]

'Also, the Jubilee Medal "Twenty Years Since the Victory in the Great Patriotic War". Also the Jubilee Medal Instituted on the Centennial of Lenin. Also the Jubilee Medal "Thirty Years Since the Victory in the Great Patriotic War". The Order "El Libertador" from Venezuela. The Great Girdle of the National Order of Upper Volta. The Great Star Order of Yugoslavia. Also the Memorial Plaquette of Belgrade City. The Great Girdle of the National Order of the Leopard from Zaire. Also the Order "Great Friend of Freedom", Great Commander, from Zambia. Also . . . '

[*'Also!'*]

'Also the Apimondia Jubilee Medal. The Gold Medal Frédéric Joliot-Curie of the World Peace Council. The Jubilee Medal of the World Federation of United Towns. The Silver Jubilee Medal issued on the 25th Anniversary of the United Nations. The Norbert Wiener Gold Medal. The Gold Medal with Sash and Plaquette of the Institute for Problems of the New International Economic Order. The Distinction "Man of the Year 1980" for Peace.'

['*He fucked the world.*'

'*He didn't fuck Israel. He didn't fuck the US.*'

'*He fucked France a lot.*'

'*France lets everyone fuck her.*'

'*He fucked the Queen of England. I can't get over that.*'

'*It was all those collars and girdles he was wearing. She couldn't see who was underneath.*'

'*He'd have to take them off to get into the bath.*'

'*Perhaps he kept them on till the last minute, then, wwwwwwwwaaaaaffffff, too late, Your Majesty.*'

'*He fucked the world.*'

'*And the world fucked him. The world fucked us.*'

'*You boys are silly. The trouble is, you're right.*'

'*Silly but right, silly but right.*'

'*What do you mean, Vera?*'

'*Those two keep saying we've been fucked. We have, against our will, over and over again. The whole country. What we need is therapy. Do you think a whole country can get therapy?*'

'*It doesn't work like that. You've just got to be prepared to be fucked by the next person instead.*'

'*Yeah, Uncle Sam with his stars-and-stripes prick.*'

'*At least he gives you presents. Packs of Marlboro.*'

'*Then he fucks you.*'

'*It's better than being fucked by Brezhnev.*'

'*Anything's better than that. The way he used to keep his boots on in bed. He simply didn't know how sensitive a girl can be.*'

'*God, you boys are so cynical.*'

'We need therapy, Vera, that's our problem.'
'Or another beer.'
'Shh. Look at this bit.']

'I was born an orphan. I was brought up under the fascist monarchy. I joined the Union of Communist Youth. I was persecuted by the bourgeois-landlord police. I served my sentence in Varkova prison. "He who has learned in the tough school of Varkova will never give up the cause of Socialism and Communism." I shed blood for my country in the Anti-Fascist Struggle. I have been helmsman of this nation for thirty-three years. Unemployment has been abolished. Inflation has been controlled by scientific methods. The Fascists have been routed. Peace has been uninterrupted. Prosperity has increased. Under my guidance, this country has grown in international stature.

'And now I find myself in a very strange position.' The red light winked on camera 2, and Petkanov turned with avuncular ease to address the nation directly. 'I find myself in court. I am charged with bringing peace and prosperity and international respect to this country. I am charged with uprooting Fascism, with abolishing unemployment, with building schools and hospitals and hydro-electric dams. I am charged with being a Socialist and a Communist. Guilty, comrades, in every case.'

He took a pause there, and let his eye drift around the court. 'Comrades,' he repeated. 'Yes, that is another strange thing. For wherever I look nowadays I see old comrades. People who swore their loyalty to the Party, who pronounced themselves true Communists, who asked for the support of the Party in their careers, who were educated, fed and clothed by Socialism, but who have now decided, in the expediency of the moment and for their own personal advantage, that they were not after all the Socialists and Communists that they once proudly maintained they were.

'Well, then, I plead guilty to sacrificing my life to improve that of the workers and peasants of our great nation. And as I said at the start of this . . . this television show for the American networks, I have been here before. I shall conclude not with my own words, but with the testimony of others. I read into the record of the court the following statements.

'Queen Elizabeth of England: "We in Great Britain today are impressed with the resolute stand you have taken in supporting this independence. Your personality, Mr President, as a statesman of world-wide repute, experience and influence, is widely acknowledged."

'Margaret Thatcher, Prime Minister of Great Britain . . . '

Solinsky was on his feet. 'Mr President of the Court, do we really . . . '

Petkanov cut off the Prosecutor General as he had so many times silenced the boy's father at meetings of the Politburo. He addressed the bench with a bullying politeness. 'You have graciously allowed me one hour. I am not supposed to mention our agreement to this effect. I am supposed to pretend that I do not wish to speak for longer than that time. You have given me an hour. I shall take it.'

'It is precisely because of such behaviour', replied the judge, 'that a limit has been imposed. You have one hour to make legal submissions and legal arguments.'

'That is what I am doing, precisely. Margaret Thatcher, Prime Minister of Great Britain . . . ' Petkanov looked up aggressively at the President, who gave a weary nod, took off his watch and placed it in front of him. 'Margaret

Thatcher: "I was impressed by the personality of the President and I am left with particular impressions about him as leader of a country willing to develop her co-operation with other nations."

'Richard Nixon: "By his so profound understanding of the world's major problems, the President can contribute and does contribute to the settlement of mankind's most urgent global problems."

'President Jimmy Carter: "The President's influence in the international arena as leader is outstanding. Thanks to her President's steady position and her independence, his country is able to act as a bridge between nations with profoundly diverging standpoints and interests, and between leaders who would otherwise have found it difficult to negotiate with one another."

'Andreas Papandreou: "The President is not only a great leader, an outstanding politician of the Balkans and of Europe, but also a front-ranking personality of the world."

'Carl Gustav XVI, King of Sweden: "You have come to symbolise the progress made by your country in the last decades. With great interest we witness the way in which your country, under your leadership, has traversed an impressive economic development."

'Juan Carlos, King of Spain: "You, Mr President, have proved, on many occasions, an active, untiring dedication to the cause of *détente*, to the safeguarding of all people's inalienable right to decide their destiny, on the path serving best their interests, to the full use of their own resources – free from the foreign interference that opposes the exertion of their own sovereignty."

'Valéry Giscard d'Estaing: "France is glad to receive the

Head of State who has had an important role in the policy of rapprochement and co-operation between the two parts of Europe."

'James Callaghan, Prime Minister of Great Britain: "You make an important contribution to the development of relations with the third world, to the efforts made for doing away with underdevelopment, to economic stability in which all the countries, the highly industrialised ones included, are interested."

'Giulio Andreotti: "I appreciate the President's role in international life will keep being positive, since he enjoys a high prestige and universal consideration thanks to his goodwill and wish for peace and for contributing to a settlement in the mutual interest."

'Franz Josef Strauss: "The leader makes an important contribution to maintaining peace, through a perspicacious policy of wide opening, through a clear assessment of the problems, through wise decisions and actions."

'Leonid Brezhnev: "The Soviet working people assess highly the wonderful gains of the working class, the co-operative peasants and the intelligentsia in your country that, under the trusted leadership of the Communist Party, have changed the look of the nation. We are glad to see that your Socialist Republic is a country developing at a fast rate, that it has a modern, developing industry and a well-organised co-operative agriculture. The activity of your entire Party, with you at the head, takes the country to new peaks of socialist construction."

'Javier Perez de Cuellaer, UN Secretary General: "I take it as a satisfaction to thank such a personality as the President for the active, constructive and energetic contribution made in all the domains of activity of the UN."

124

'Mario Soares: "For myself, I highly appreciate the efforts of the President in favour of European security, of all people's peace and independence, of non-interference by some countries in other countries' domestic affairs."

'Prince Norodom Sihanouk: "Your socialist nation and her much beloved leader, who internationally symbolise, in a wonderful way, the firm attachment to the ideas of justice, freedom, independence, peace and progress, are always on the side of the oppressed peoples, those that are victims of aggression and that fight to win their independence back."

'Hu Yuobang, General Secretary of the Central Committee of the Chinese Communist Party: "You safeguard firmly the state sovereignty and national dignity. In international activity, you are against the law of force, you safeguard the peace of the world and the cause of human progress."

'President Canaan Banana of Zimbabwe: "You have understood that your independence cannot be complete unless the whole of mankind is freed from the chains of imperialism and colonialism. That is why your country has stood at the forefront of those who have assisted us in our just struggle for national emancipation. You have given us material and moral support in the hardest of trials."

'Mohammad Hosni Mubarak, President of the Arab Republic of Egypt: "As to myself, I experience the same joy about our relationship, a joy stemming from my profound appreciation of your clear-sighted position, of your wisdom, courage, wide, all-embracing vision of history, of your particular capability of assuming responsibility, of your standing above events and your approach to the realities of the epoch." '

[*'He fucked them all. He really fucked them all.'*
*'Takes two to fuck.'*]

'I am not making these claims for myself,' Petkanov continued. 'This is what others say, others who are more competent to judge.

'When I was here before, many years ago, in the bourgeois-fascist court in Velpen, I was charged, as I am now, with invented crimes. You, Professor Prosecutor, at the start of this . . . show, reminded me that the crimes I was accused of as a sixteen-year-old member of the Union of Communist Youth were listed as damage to property and so on. But everyone knew that I was really charged with the capital offence of being a Socialist and a Communist, of wishing to improve the lot of working people and the peasants. Everyone knew that, the bourgeois-landlord police, the prosecutor, the court, myself and my comrades. And everyone knew that this is what I was sentenced for.

'And the same is happening again. Everyone, everyone in this court and who is a witness to this show, knows that the charges against me are convenient inventions. I was the helmsman of this nation for thirty-three years, I was a Communist, I sacrificed my whole life for the people, therefore I must be a criminal according to those who once made the same promises and swore the same oaths that they now betray. But the real charge, which we all know, is that I am a Socialist and a Communist, and that I am proud to be a Socialist and a Communist. So let us not beat about the bush, my former comrades. I plead guilty to the real charge. Now sentence me to whatever it is that you have already decided.'

With a final, belligerent glare at his accusers, Stoyo Petkanov abruptly sat down. The President of the Court glanced at his watch. One hour and seven minutes.

*

By late February the last legal submissions were being made. Sun was beginning to pierce the smog over the city. Granny March would soon be here. She was known to be a capricious old woman, and very hard to please, but when she smiled, she promised you fine weather.

Peter Solinsky had bought two *martenitsas*: woollen tassels, each of them half red and half white. Red and white chased away evil, brought good luck and good health. But this year Maria didn't want to hang them up.

'We hung them up last year. Every year.'

'Last year I loved you. Last year I respected you.'

Peter Solinsky phoned for a taxi. Well, if that was how it was going to be. At least one of the new freedoms was that you didn't have to fake gratitude about being married to the daughter of a leading anti-Fascist. *She* should have been grateful to *him* instead of disparaging his performance, calling him a TV lawyer. Even if the court had subsequently declined to add the charge of murder to the indictment, he had done well, very well. Everyone told him so. His *coup de théâtre* had shifted public perception decisively. Newspaper cartoons portrayed him as St Georgi slaying the dragon. The faculty of law had given a dinner in his honour. Women smiled at him now, even women he didn't know. His only critics had been Maria, the editorialists at *Truth*, and the author of an anonymous postcard he had received the other day. The picture showed the former Communist Party headquarters in Sliven, and the text simply read: GIVE US CONVICTIONS NOT JUSTICE!

He asked the taxi driver to take him to the northern hills.

'Saying goodbye, Chief?'

'Goodbye?' Did it show that he'd just had a row with Maria?

'To Alyosha. I hear they're carting him away.'

'Do you think that's a good idea?'

'Comrade Chief.' The driver pronounced the words with obvious irony. He turned slightly towards his passenger, but all Solinsky could see was a wizened neck, a battered cap and the profile of a half-smoked cigarette. 'Comrade Chief, now that we're all free and can speak our minds, permit me to inform you that I don't give a fuck either way.'

The taxi parked and waited for him. He walked up through the public gardens and climbed the granite steps. For a little longer Alyosha would continue to raise his glittering bayonet and advance hopefully into the future; around his plinth the machine-gunners would go on holding whatever position they had been set to defend. And then? Would something else go up in Alyosha's place, or had the time for monuments passed?

Peter Solinsky looked down over the bare chestnuts and limes, the poplars and the walnuts, all weeks away from leaf. To the west he could see Rykosha Mountain, the scene of Petkanov's adolescent rhapsody (or banal fabrication). To the south lay the smogbound city, guarded by its domestic ramparts. Friendship 1, Friendship 2, Friendship 3, Friendship 4 . . . Perhaps he should get a new place to live, as Maria had suggested. He could mention it to the Deputy Minister of Housing, who like him had been an early member of the Green Party. Just because Maria wasn't coming with him, it didn't mean he had to live in a dingy mouse-hole. Six rooms, perhaps? A prosecutor general sometimes has to receive foreign dignitaries at home. And then, well, he wouldn't be divorced for ever.

He remembered standing here as a boy, stiff-backed beside his father, hearing the band, watching the Soviet

Ambassador lay a wreath and salute. He remembered Stoyo Petkanov ripe with power. Anna Petkanova too: the pug face, the braided hair. For the next ten years or so, he'd had a distant crush on the Beacon of Youth. The magazine photos had made her look stylish, and she'd been interested in jazz. Had she really been murdered? Had the country been that degraded? Would anyone do anything for any reason? Who could tell. Stalin had Kirov murdered: welcome to the modern world.

Coming down the granite steps, Peter Solinsky took the two *martenitsas* out of his raincoat pocket. He crossed a patch of scruffy grass, and beneath the approving gaze of three aged municipal gardeners, slipped the woollen tassels under a large stone. That's what you did in the country at this time of year. A few days later you would go back to where you had left the *martenitsa*. If there were ants under the stone, there would be lambs on the farm that year; worms and bugs meant horses and cattle; spiders stood for donkeys. Any living thing that stirred promised you fertility, a new beginning.

*

'How was your weekend, Peter? Has anything happened? Did the mental defectives hold a protest against the new constitution?'

This man was indefatigable. You couldn't understand him because he kept exhausting you. It must be all that yoghurt he ate. Or the wild geranium under his bed. Good health and long life: the plant of centenarians. Perhaps he should order the militiaman to chuck it out of the window the next time Petkanov left the room.

The Prosecutor General no longer felt like jousting. The case was over except for the sentence, and he had won. Strange that the defendant had shown him no ill-will – or at least, no extra ill-will – after the allegations about Anna Petkanova. Or perhaps that told you something.

'I went to see my father,' Peter Solinsky replied.

'And how is he?'

'He is dying, as I told you.'

'Well, there are no bears in the ground. Truly, I am sorry. Whatever our differences . . . '

Solinsky did not want to hear another grotesque and sentimental perversion of his family's past. 'My father talked about you,' he said sharply. Petkanov looked across in anticipation, a leader accustomed to flattery. But his expectant mood dwindled as he studied the prosecutor's face: thin, harsh, older. No, he couldn't call him a boy any more. 'My father did not have many words left, but he wanted me to hear them. He said that when you were young, when you were both young, you were a true believer. Oh, he said you were crazy for power, but that wasn't incompatible with being a true believer. He said he wondered at what point you lost the faith. It worried him, to know when and how it happened. Perhaps at the death of your daughter, but perhaps, he thought, long, long before.'

'You may tell your father that I am still a true believer in Socialism and Communism. I have never wavered from the path.'

'Then you will be interested in what my father said to me, just before I left. He said, "I have a riddle for you, Peter. Which is worse, the true believer who continues to believe despite all the evidence of observable reality; or the person who admits such reality yet continues to claim to be a true believer?" '

Stoyo Petkanov for once tried not to show all of his exasperation. That was just like old Solinsky, always trying to play the fucking intellectual. There they would be, in the final stages of approving the next economic programme, with ministers worrying about targets set, or the rains at harvest-time, or the effect of yet another crisis in the Middle East on Mother Russia's supply of crude, and old Solinsky would fiddle with his pipe and push back his chair and pompously spout theory. 'Comrades, I have been re-reading . . . ' was his favourite way of starting to bore them. *Re*-reading! You read, of course, to begin with, you studied, but then you worked, you acted. The scientific principles of Socialism were laid down, and you applied them. Of course with local variations. But when you were deciding the completion date for the hydro-electric dam, or wondering why the peasants in the north-east were withholding grain, or considering the DIS's report on the ethnic Hungarian minority, you did not, Mr Comrade Doctor Professor Fucking Solinsky, if you don't mind my saying, you did not, excuse me, need to *re*-read anything. His trouble was that he had been far too soft, far too patient with Peter's father. The old fool should have been sent to the country to play with his bees years earlier. He hadn't been so high and mighty and theoretical when they'd been in Varkova prison together. He hadn't asked the warders permission to re-read something before laying into that Iron Guard who'd become detached from the main group. Solinsky had known how to make a Fascist whimper in those days.

But the former President did not express any of this. Instead, in a quiet voice, he said, 'Every man has doubts. It is normal. Perhaps there were times when even I did not believe. But I allowed others to. Can *you* do as much?'

'Ah,' replied the prosecutor. 'The great enabler. The flawed priest who leads the ignorant to Heaven.'

'Your words.'

\*

'He's guilty, Granny.'

Stefan's grandmother stirred her head slightly, and looked up from beneath her woollen cap at the student's face. The silly little thrush, grinning stupidly, twitching his beak up at the colour portrait of V.I. Lenin.

'They found your sweetheart guilty as well, Granny. While they were at it.'

'So are you happy?'

The thrush was startled by her sudden question. He thought for a moment, then exhaled his cigarette smoke over the founder of the Soviet State. 'Yes,' he said, 'now you ask. I'm blissed.'

'Then I pity you.'

'Why?' For the first time the boy seemed to concentrate properly on the old woman sitting beneath her icon. But she had turned her eyes away from him and retreated into her memories. 'Why?' he repeated.

'God forbid that a blind man should learn to see.'

\*

Vera, Atanas, Stefan and Dimiter turned off the television and went out for a beer. They sat in a smoky café which had been a bookshop before the Changes.

'What do you think he'll get?'

'*Takka-takka-takka.*'

'No, they won't do that.'

The beers arrived. Silently, reverently, they raised their glasses and clunked them damply together. The past, the future, the end of things, the beginning of things. They each drank a serious first mouthful.

'So, anyone here feel purged?'

'Atanas, you're such a cynic.'

'Me? A cynic? I'm so uncynical I just wanted them to put him up against a wall and shoot him.'

'There had to be a trial. They couldn't just say, off you go, we'll pretend you're sick. That's what the Communists used to do.'

'It wasn't right, though, was it, the trial? What he's done to the country, you can't just put it in criminal terms. It should have been about more, about how he corrupted everything he touched. Everything we touch too. The land, the grass, the stones. How he lied all the time, automatically, as a policy, as a reflex, and how he taught everyone else to. How people can't trust easily any more. How he corrupted even the words that come out of our mouths.'

'He didn't corrupt mine, the lying fucking shit-faced dog-eating bastard.'

'Atanas, I wish you'd be serious. Just once.'

'I thought that was part of it, Vera.'

'Part of what?'

'Freedom. Freedom not to be serious. Not ever again. Not ever, ever, if you don't want to be. Isn't that my right, to be frivolous for the rest of my life if I want to be?'

'Atanas, you were just as frivolous before the Changes.'

'Then it was anti-social behaviour. Hooliganism. Now it's my constitutional right.'

'Is this what we've been fighting for? Atanas's right to be frivolous?'

'Perhaps that's enough to be going on with for the moment.'

*

The day before the sentence in Criminal Law Case Number I was published, Peter Solinsky came to see Stoyo Petkanov for the last time. The old man was standing inside the painted semicircle with his nose to the window. The militiaman on duty had been instructed that the restriction no longer applied. Let him see the view now if he wished. Let him look down over the city he had once bossed.

They sat on opposite sides of the deal table while Petkanov read through the court's decision as if searching for an irregularity. Thirty years of internal exile. That should see him out. Personal assets sequestered by the State. Something familiar, almost comforting about that. Well, he had begun with nothing, he would end with nothing. He shrugged and put the paper down.

'You have not stripped me of my medals and honours.'

'We thought you should keep them.'

Petkanov grunted. 'So, anyway, how are you, Peter?' Now he was grinning at the prosecutor with a crazy fullness, as if life were just about to begin, a life studded with jaunts and schemes and madcap ventures.

'How am I?' Exhausted, for one thing. If this was the sour-stomached, thick-brained weariness you felt when you had got what you wanted, when your country had been liberated and your professional career kissed with success, what was the weariness of defeat like? That initial sense of triumph was now emptied bathwater. 'How am I? Since

134

you ask, my father is dead, my wife wants a divorce and my daughter is refusing to speak to me. How would you expect me to be?'

Petkanov grinned again, and light glinted on the metal of his spectacles. He felt strangely cheerful. He had lost everything, but he was less defeated than this ageing young man. Intellectuals were pathetic, he had always known it. Probably young Solinsky would now decline into illness. How he despised those who got sick. 'Well, Peter, you must reflect that your changed circumstances now give you more time to devote to the salvation of your country.'

Was he being ironic? Trying to claim some bond between them, giving him advice like this? Peter's thin consolation was the knowledge that he loathed this man as much as ever. He rose to leave; but the former President had not quite finished with him. Despite his age, he moved swiftly round the table, shook the prosecutor's hand, and then sandwiched it between his own plump paws.

'Tell me, Peter,' he asked, in a voice that was both sarcastic and ingratiating, 'do you think me a monster?'

'I don't care.' Solinsky was keen only to get away.

'Well, let me put it this way. Do you think of me as an ordinary man, or as a monster?'

'Neither.' The Prosecutor General gave a sharp nasal sigh. 'I suppose I think of you as just a gangster.'

Petkanov laughed unexpectedly at this. 'That is not answering my question. Peter, let me give you a riddle, to replace the one your father gave you. Either I am a monster or I am not. Yes? If I am not, then I must be someone like you, or someone you might be capable of becoming. Which do you want me to be? It is up to you to decide.'

When Solinsky declined to answer, the former President

135

pressed on, almost tauntingly. 'No, you are not interested? Then let me continue. If I am a monster, I will come back to haunt your dreams, I will be your nightmare. If I am like you, I will come back to haunt your living days. Which do you prefer? Eh?'

Now Petkanov was tugging on his hand, pulling him closer so that Solinsky could smell hard-boiled egg on his breath. 'You cannot get rid of me. This farce of a trial makes no difference. Killing me would make no difference. Lying about me, saying I was only hated and feared, not loved, that will make no difference. You can't get rid of me. Do you see?'

The Prosecutor General wrenched his hand from his captor's grasp. He felt stained, contaminated, sexually corrupted, irradiated to the bone marrow. 'To hell with you,' he shouted, turning violently away. He found himself face to face with the young militiaman, who was following the exchange with a new democratic curiosity. Something made the prosecutor nod politely, and the soldier clicked his heels in response. Then he shouted again, 'To hell with you. Curse you.'

As he was reaching for the doorknob he heard a dry scuttle behind him. He was startled by the terror he felt. A hand gripped his upper arm and made him turn. The former President was now glaring up at him, and pulling, pulling to bring their faces closer. Suddenly, the prosecutor lost strength, and their eyes were furiously on the same level.

'No,' said Stoyo Petkanov. 'You are wrong. I curse you. I sentence you.' The unvanquished stare, the whiff of hard-boiled egg, the old fingers clamped bruisingly around the upper arm. '*I* sentence *you*.'

*

136

Since the Changes, people had started coming back to the Church; not just for baptism and burial, but for worship, for unspecific consolation, for the knowledge that they were more than bees in a hive. Peter Solinsky had expected a crush of head-scarved *babas*, but he saw only men and women, young and old and middle-aged: people like himself. He stood awkwardly in the narthex of St Sophia, feeling like an impostor, wondering what to do, whether to genuflect. When no-one challenged his credentials, he began to walk slowly up the narrow side aisle. He had left behind the dull forty watts of a March afternoon; now his eyes adjusted to a brightness that depended upon surrounding darkness. Candles blazed at him, the polished brass was fiery, and small high windows focused the sun into thin hard rays.

The sturdy wrought-iron candle-stand, with its bristling spikes and soft curlicues, was a theatre of light. Candles were lit at two levels: at shoulder height for the living, ankle height for the dead. Peter Solinsky bought two beeswax tapers and touched them into flame. He knelt, and pressed the first one into the flat tray of sand on the church floor. Then he rose, extended his arm, and forced the base of the second candle, the one burning for his country, down on to a black iron spike. The assembled flames were hot on his face. He retreated stiffly, like a wreath-laying general, and stood to attention. Then his fingertip discovered his forehead, and unprotestingly he continued the sempiternal gesture, crossing himself, from right to left, in the Orthodox fashion.

*

137

Evening and rain fell softly together. On a low hill to the north of the city stood a concrete pedestal, sullen and aimless. The bronze panels round its sides gleamed dully in the damp. Without Alyosha to lead them into the future, the machine-gunners now found themselves fighting a different battle: irrelevant, local, silent.

On the piece of waste ground beside the marshalling yard, rain gave a gentle sweat to Lenin and Stalin, to Brezhnev, to the First Leader, and to Stoyo Petkanov. Spring was coming, and the first tendrils would soon try once again to take a hold on the skiddy bronze of military boots. In the dark, locomotives lurched on wet points and dragged at overhead cables, flashing brief light on to sculpted faces. But argument had ceased in this posthumous Politburo; the stiff giants had fallen silent.

In front of the vacant Mausoleum of the First Leader an old woman stood alone. She wore a woollen scarf wrapped round a woollen hat, and both were soaked. In outstretched fists she held a small framed print of V.I. Lenin. Rain bubbled the image, but his indelible face pursued each passer-by. Occasionally, a committed drunk or some chattering thrush of a student would shout across at the old woman, at the thin light veering off the wet glass. But whatever the words, she stood her ground, and she remained silent.